Sozwik

by Stephen Parato

In the weeks leading up to the freeing, a solemn group of seven Jyoti repeatedly met with the servants of The Guard.

During these meetings, they were told that "freedom is mandatory." This was The Guard's deceptive way of saying that once granted freedom, they had to completely comply with the rules of freedom. In other words, accept leaving Seren forever, or else…

The instructions were as expected. Like the preceding generation, they would be sent to Earth to live out the rest of their lives.

It was also made crystal clear that they were not to interfere with human affairs, at all. The Guard's vague threat was mysteriously forewarning: Any interaction with humans would result in punishment far worse than physical death.

This tale follows the journey of one of those Jyoti… Sozwik, son of Anda and Macha, and student of Goa.

Chapter 1
The Departure

On the hilltop, so far removed from the underground caverns, Sozwik found himself reluctantly relieved.

The landscape exhibited an intense openness. The fresh air, running through his hair, felt like being birthed into an entirely new world. For Sozwik, leaving would have been more difficult if he had a choice. But his hands were tied.

Sozwik had earned his 'freedom'.

After a lifetime of forced slavery inside the zapixion mines, he had achieved what so few had been able to do. Sozwik toiled his way up to Top Rank, the highest position a Jyoti could obtain, and was the youngest yet to do so.

Just seven Jyoti of each generation were granted freedom. And only those of Top Rank were even eligible. Freedom was a fleeting dream that so many clung to, yet such a small number would ever taste. The leading theory was that this was done for two reasons… The first, to provide desperate, (almost) unattainable hope for the masses. The second was to stifle any possibility of rebellion by shipping the potential leaders off.

The craft appeared out of the peaceful purple sky, silhouetted by the omnipresent rays of the Great Star. It landed on the square, dull metallic platform, mere meters from the group of seven.

The group bowed their heads, joining the entire Jyoti race in a final goodbye. A soothing invocation that was unspoken, yet directly experienced, connecting thousands of kindred spirits in reverence.

An abrupt bark snapped the silence. "Move!" The gold-armored guards grunted through their gnarled, steel blue jaws. Their staffs were as menacing as their eyes. And both were bitterly fixated on the Jyoti as the seven began to walk up the gray loading ramp and onto the ship.

"Until next life... fuck heads," Sozwik jokingly communicated. The other six produced a slight smirk because, of course, the guards couldn't possibly hear it.

Aboard the craft, they were greeted by the all-too-familiar hostile presence of another gang of guards. The Jyoti had learned to live with it and became comfortable with being constantly uncomfortable.

It was Sozwik's first time in a craft. The metallic hull was like the insides of a monstrous beast. Curved beams lined the sides and looped around an immense, concave ceiling. The floors were smooth, solid silver, giving the interior a cold disposition. There were eight authoritative red security doors, laid out symmetrically, that led to the more comfortable rooms and the pilot station. The Jyoti could only imagine the extravagant luxuries that these rooms held.

After a short stint of standing in the hull, Sozwik felt a sudden pressure in his legs. The craft had left the ground. For the first time in his life, Sozwik ascended out of the blanket-like atmosphere of Seren, his home planet.

Time and space seemed to do funny things. Sozwik felt a chronological slowing, similar to the times he and his friends would play the game of Downhill, where they would race down steep inclines at breakneck speed, dodging immense trees and hopping over boulders. His feet would move too fast to even think. But he was in a different zone, where he had an eternity to pinpoint each step. Now he had that feeling again within the craft.

Before he could even metabolize the experience, they were overlooking the most captivating planet — a blue-green orb, with white swirls that looked like paint strokes, hanging in suspended animation amidst the brilliant blackness of the universe.

"Earth," the seven Jyoti communicated in unison.

Their eyes were utterly infatuated, in awe of the heavenly body that dominated the view from the craft's window.

"Enjoy your freedom." The guards snickered in a sarcastic, brutish tone, as the Jyoti were beamed to different remote areas on the planet.

In his consciousness, Sozwik revisited his last night on Seren as the blue-white light engulfed him.

Chapter 2
The Night Before the Freeing

The night before the freeing a celebratory feast was held in the village center.

Feasts were allowed only once per year by The Guard, so these festivities were thoroughly enjoyed and cherished.

The Jyoti resided within the bounds of a valley, surrounded by mountains on all sides. What was once a comforting collective sanctuary was now an open-air prison where they were forced, day in and day out, to work inside the zapixion mines embedded inside the belly of the mountains.

The village was an interwoven treehouse complex which wound through the forestry of the valley. The Jyoti had a knack for building in such a way that everything became a seamless extension of nature. When viewed from above, it would be nearly impossible to tell that a highly advanced civilization inhabited the valley. This symbiotic relationship with nature acted as the root of the Jyoti's existence, the blooming of their culture and the seeds of their strength.

Gardens hugged the base of almost every tree, making the ground a meandering river of vibrantly colored vegetation. Besides that, you would have to look up to see any housing structures.

Since the Jyoti are expert climbers, getting into a treehouse was almost as easy as walking. Some of the eldest Jyoti, however, used vine ropes to maneuver up and down from their homes.

At the very heart of the village lay a field, bright and lively green, with no classifiable shape, as is the unpredictable nature of nature. The Jyoti often used such open spaces as the center from which to build villages around, like a natural version of the village squares built on Earth.

One colossal table — The Grand Table — took residence in the revered field in the center of the village. It was a raw sienna colored, curving piece of wood, mimicking the spiral-sequence which pervades all of nature. The table's centermost point was the trunk of the most brobdingnagian tree, and it unwound outward in larger and larger spirals. The sacred geometry of the feast table made it a powerful amplifier of energy, which is why it was used for jubilant celebration.

The Jyoti kept a keen eye on the patterns that manifested in nature, from the smallest of flowers to the most expansive of galaxies. It was believed that harmonizing with these inherent patterns would bring harmony to their lives. This is why, despite several generations of slavery, the Jyoti were able to maintain a deep sense of pride and a certain spiritual lightheartedness that the servants of The Guard scathingly envied.

Sozwik sat cross-legged near the center of the gigantic spiral. The Top Rank lined the interior of the center of the spiral table, with their relatives opposite them on the outside. Being the youngest of the Top Rank, Sozwik was the only one to not yet have a family of his own. His parents sat opposite him, still strong and always tremendously dependable. Both had dark brown hair covering the entirety of their bodies, with highlights of gray wisdom strands. They were beaming as they took their seats opposite Sozwik, noticeably proud of the fact that Sozwik had earned his freedom, even though they knew it wouldn't be the "happily ever after" scenario that most of the village believed.

Ω

Sozwik's mother, Anda, was widely revered in the Jyoti community as the best designstress on Seren. She had such knowledge of sacred universal patterns and an uncanny feel for the energy of trees. Anda had in fact played a pivotal role in the design of The Grand Table.

Macha, Sozwik's father, was one of the largest Jyoti on Seren. He was known as "The Jyoti Jester," as he tended to leave a path of hysterically laughing Jyoti wherever he went. Macha's whole generation credits him with making their mining work tolerable, as he had a bottomless reservoir of playful wit to draw from.

Sozwik, now a well wisened Jyoti himself, thoroughly enjoyed his parents' company. Though there was still that subtle pull of parental expectation, he would probably have gotten along with them even if he were not their only son.

Ω

The feast included a diverse array of the most delicious foods. Vegetables, fruits, and berries were piled on the table in gigantic wooden bowls. Dozens of different homemade herbal dipping sauces formed grand lines of saucers, amplifying the appetizing aroma of the meal.

Each and every Jyoti had a hand in creating the feast. Their old adage — which was always delivered with a half-laugh — was, "If everyone does a little bit, no one has to do a lot."

Every Jyoti also had a beautifully sculpted, customized wooden chalice. Hand-crafting his or her own unique chalice was a rite of passage for the Jyoti. The chalices were all filled with Krit, the Jyoti's celebratory ceremonial beverage. Krit was made from fermented tree sap, combined with the juices of several medicine plants. It was a light intoxicant, mild entheogen and healing tonic all-in-one. Because it was regarded as sacred, Krit was only drunk on special occasions.

Once every Jyoti's cup was poured, the entire village simultaneously went into silence and closed their eyes. After a collective dip in the dazzling darkness of the void, they opened their eyes and raised their glasses to the treetops in beautiful unison. After a few moments, the gathering erupted in a roar of laughter, filling the valley with a pleasant mist of colorful enchantment.

So goes the Jyoti's collective Kritual.

The jubilant laughter slowly transitioned back to conversation along the full circumvolution of The Grand Table.

"To Sozwik," Macha proudly said as his chalice formed a holy triangle with Sozwik and Anda's.

As Sozwik lifted his chalice of Krit to his lips, he caught a glimpse of Goa, his mentor and legendary Wakan Master, playfully winking at him, two spirals out and slightly to the left. In response, Sozwik telepathically communicated the sacred flower of life symbol and smiled. Then he dropped back into conversation with his parents.

The mood was merry, as it tended to be with Macha around (except when he was angry, but that's rare for any Jyoti, including Macha).

"I'm proud of you," said Anda, looking at her son with adoration.

"Not so much with the whole Top Rank thing," Macha interrupted with a grin. "But because you're wisened enough to see through the illusion."

Anda continued. "Goa has trained you well. You're capable enough to handle any situation you encounter. I can tell you that much. Like we've all discussed, only you will know what you can actually do once you're on Earth. Though I have a feeling something unforeseen will find you."

"Couldn't have said it better myself." Macha exclaimed.

After the food was eaten, the entire tribe raised their chalices again, and this time, partook in ritual song. The valley filled with harmonized hymns between hundreds of Jyoti, accompanied by the swaggered percussion of wood-knocking on the grand table.

Another Jyoti rite of passage was the crafting of a hefty knock-stick. Like the chalices, each knock-stick was unique. Because every Jyoti was learned in both vocal harmony and percussion at an early age (one of the few traditions that withstood the woes of enslavement), the cohesive sound of the whole tribe was something to behold. Harmonies spontaneously transitioned to smaller groups breaking into different melodies, like an ever-evolving, super-organism of sound. There were even individual harmonies that took the lead at times for a short solo soliloquy. It was a magical dance of aural delight.

From an Earthly perspective, the sound could be described as the intersection between Native American tribal songs, Tibetan Buddhist chanting and the smooth, interplaying melodies of an acapella group.

The energy was palpable. Sozwik took a deep inhale through his wide, flaring nostrils and felt bliss fill his entire being, like water pouring into a chalice.

The melodic sounds reverberated through the valley as the last streams of sunlight trickled over the purple-hued mountains. In the dreamy dance of dusk, day passed the baton to night and Seren was slowly steeped in darkness.

Ω

The event ended and everyone parted ways, heading home for the night.

Sozwik and his parents slowly walked along the meandering path which led to the base of their tree house complex, as if trying to slow the flow of time.

"A Jyoti feast done right," Macha proclaimed.

"Indeed," Sozwik replied, as they all intuitively stopped and turned to face each other.

Macha continued…

"Us Wakan are not only the bridge between the physical and unseen realms. We're also the instigators of trouble. The good kind of trouble. Trouble for all of those who seek control over others. We each have our role in the Grand Unfoldment. Our role (motioning to himself and Anda) lies here on Seren. But yours, Sozwik, awaits you on Earth."

Sozwik nodded his head in hesitant agreement.

"It's difficult not knowing exactly what your role is," Anda said in a comforting tone. "As uncertainty prevails in this time. But uncertainty is the sister of change. And your purpose will be further revealed to you as you meet it halfway."

"We have faith in you Sozwik," parents said in unison, as if they both channeled the message from the same source. "And we're always here for you, always sending our love, no matter what. Remember that."

"Even if you do something crazy like marry one of them humans right under The Guard's nose," Macha added to lighten the mood. They all laughed away the heavy weight of anxiety as they slowly strolled together.

Stopping at the foot of the marvelous tree that housed Anda and Macha's charming wooden home, they shared a moment of connected silence and embraced each other.

"I love you," the family of three said together and relished in each other's physical presence for what may very well be the last time. Sozwik would be aboard the craft by first light.

With a gentle sweep, Sozwik placed each of his hands on his parents' shoulders. Then he slowly turned away and traipsed towards his own treehouse. Each step created a tighter pulling on his heartstrings.

"I need their strength," Sozwik confessed in a state of self-admitted helplessness.

Ω

Sozwik poignantly felt a shadow of anxiety lurking, creeping in. He stood in the center of his open-space treehouse — whose center column was a gargantuan Tontak tree — overwhelmed by the bittersweet nostalgia of it all. He built it himself, next to his parents' home. The trees who held their abodes were mighty brothers of compassionate spirit, standing side by side. Sozwik's space held a familiar, loving energy. It was the ultimate soother of the mind.

The whole wooden structure — which replicated the curving, squiggles of nature — seemed to smile at him. His mammoth hammock draped from the ceiling, gently caressing the nearby wall like the consoling touch of a mother's hand on the forehead of an infant. His wooden staff, embedded with golden Wakan symbolism of old, seemed to wink at him in a gesture of playful respect as it coolly leaned against the wall.

This was Sozwik's home, his place of refuge, infused with a grounded joviality from years of ritual meditation, dance and celebration of life. But now an aloof detachment was wedged between him and his sacred space. He prepped his mind to leave at first light.

Sozwik found his fate difficult to accept, although the thought of freedom was enticing. And if he were to disobey The Guard's orders, the entire Jyoti race would suffer the consequences. Recognizing this, Sozwik made peace with his situation and, with reluctance, climbed out of his home.

He felt a calling. It was subtle, yet unavoidable, and all-too-familiar. The source could be none other than…

"Goa must be reaching out to me through the ethers," Sozwik thought. He made his way to their secret meeting spot – a small, open grove. It was bright green and enchanting by day, and dark green and mystical by night. Sozwik walked as stealthy as Jyoti-ly possible (which is stealthier than 99.9% of beings in the Universe), trying to reach the center without Goa detecting him. It was a game of sorts that they played every time. A game Sozwik never won. Thinking he was alone, Sozwik sat with a sigh of triumphant relief.

"Ahhh!" A yelp of surprise leapt out of him as Goa seemed to materialize in front of his very eyes.

"You're thinking about the future. If you were in the now you would've sensed me from a mile off."

Embarrassed, Sozwik drooped his head and let out a dreary, "Yup…" Then continued. "You're right. But it's hard to be in the moment when I'm leaving Seren forever tomorrow. I'm scared, Goa. I'm really scared. Do you understand?"

Goa eased his tone. "Yes, I understand. And this is all the more reason to be present. Truly feel your fear, instead of pretending you're fearless all of the time. That's the trap of the masculine. Awareness is transformative. And strength lies in vulnerability."

"That is true," replied Sozwik.

Goa went on. "This is why I reached out to you. You have enough strength and wisdom, Sozwik, even more than most of the elders. That's why you were able to achieve Top Rank so quickly. You know how to play the game, and more importantly, you realize that it is a game."

Sozwik let out a soft smirk as Goa continued.

"Plus, you know more than the average Jyoti, who believe there is no telepathic communication from Earth. Your Wakan training will allow you to get at least some signal, even amidst any interference. Just be subtle, like I've taught you. What we do, as Wakan, must be nurtured in the unseen, like a seed that holds much potential for change."

"Yes," Sozwik nodded.

Goa now gave Sozwik a more serious look. "You have much potential as well, Sozwik, but remember that you're an intrinsic part of a greater whole. You can't do everything yourself. You can be quite so stubborn, Sozwik. That's why I had to reach out to you tonight, otherwise you would have tried to handle everything yourself, unaware of your blind spots. But I can see you in a way you cannot see yourself. And you can do the same for me, as you've beautifully demonstrated many times."

Goa paused for a moment, making sure Sozwik got the message. "It's okay to ask for help, Sozwik. Remember that. We live in a co-creative universe. We're all in this together and we can all help each other. Just use your discernment to know who has good intentions and who doesn't."

"I will remember that." Sozwik replied, and then went on. "You're right. I have gone far solely off the strength of my own will. But soon I will be in over my head and need to stand upon the shoulders of giants in order to see. No one is an island. I'm slowly realizing that."

Goa placed his gentle hand upon Sozwik's shoulder. "You hold much wisdom, Sozwik. I am grateful to know you."

"Thank you," Sozwik answered, almost choked up by the overwhelming emotion.

The two Jyoti sat together in silence, gazing at the stars above, which looked like pearl punctures of light through the black fabric of the universe.

After several minutes, Goa broke the silence with a howling, "Ohhhhh..." It was almost comical, the way it instantly shifted the energy.

"I almost forgot to tell you this, Sozwik. The ankle bands, the Top Rank Badge, provided by The Guard, are actually tracking devices. Few know this. The Guard, being The Guard and all, is full of deception. It keeps tabs on all of the 'free' Jyoti. The Guard has a keen interest in our ways, for some reason. No one knows why. It's been speculated that it wants to figure out how to use our unseen ways for its own power."

Sozwik reacted like a rebellious teenager. "I'll just take it off then and they'll be hard-pressed to find me then." He let out a laugh of feigned confidence.

"It's not that simple." Goa said. "No one has yet figured out how to remove them. And if you do, and leave it somewhere, The Guard will know immediately, by the lack of movement and heat sensing. And there will be high alert across their domain."

Goa hummed. "But there is a solution. Some have found ways to… How can I say this? To make the signal a bit weak..."

"Yes?" Belted Sozwik with childlike curiosity. "Tell me..."

"It has been said that some of the ancient Wakan meditation techniques can temporarily interfere with the tag's signal. When you do this, The Guard will just think its equipment is a bit faulty or that you're in a very remote area. Only do this when absolutely necessary though, or The Guard will catch on to what you're doing. And who knows what kind of wrath will be carried out if it realizes it's been outsmarted."

"That's good to know," said Sozwik, grateful for the last-minute wisdom. Though in the back of his mind, he still doubted the supposed supreme technological prowess of The Guard.

"The fate of our race, the Earthlings and The Guard are now intimately woven together. We all hang in a delicate balance that only few are in a position to tip. Sozwik, you are one of them."

The realization hit Sozwik like a tidal wave and threatened to drown him. Feeling overwhelmed by this weight suddenly thrust upon him, Sozwik looked at Goa with pleading eyes. "Why me, Goa? Why me? I don't feel ready for this."

Goa, with level eyes, replied, "It is not always us that choose our destiny. Sometimes our destiny chooses us. And when it does, it's an omen that you're capable of seeing it through."

"Seeing what through?" Sozwik asked.

"I honestly don't know, Sozwik. But you soon will know. I can promise you that. I have tremendous faith in you, young Sozwik. The truth lies within you. You will discover many a thing that I don't even know.

You don't need to see the whole path, just trust that the light of The Divine will always allow you to see enough to continue moving forward. If you keep moving forward, you will eventually see the whole path."

Sozwik embraced Goa in a strong Jyoti hug, indicating that, for the moment at least, a sense of empowerment had cast out his anxieties.

They then looked each other in the eyes, and with a blend of sadness and excitement, softly chanted the "Jyoti Oneness" prayer together:

"I am you
You are me
Different waves
Same sea"

A smile danced on Goa's face that instantly leapt to Sozwik's face as well. Sozwik put his hand up to rub a tear of joy from his right eye, and by the time he had blinked, Goa was gone.

"That sly nycono," Sozwik chuckled to himself.

Ω

Nyconos are, of course, the galactically famous practical jokers. They're small nocturnal creatures native to Seren, like a combination of the foxes and raccoons of Earth. Nyconos are cunning beyond measure, even more stealthy than Jyoti (because they're smaller). They're mischievous, yet lighthearted, and infamously use their sticky fingers for all kinds of thievery and pranks.

Throughout the millennia, nyconos provided the Jyoti with plenty of both amusement and annoyance, like a wild little brother who, for better or worse, made life a bit more entertaining.

In the Wakan tradition of animal totems, nyconos represent cleverness, playfulness, and the trickster archetype. If a Jyoti caught sight of a nycono, it was a good sign, because of their stealth.

Legend has it that Goa was the secret leader of the nyconos. When asked about this, he would always just reply with a smirk.

Ω

Sozwik walked away slowly, his mind in a world of deep personal reflection, as his body meandered through the dense woodlands back towards the village. He scanned the twilight scenery until it became all of his memories. Family, friends, places, and events - all so dear to him - paid their farewells in the realm of imagination.

Ω

Sozwik saw himself looking up from what was the Jyoti equivalent of a crib. To his pleasant surprise, both of his parents' heads hovered above him, beaming with unconditional love. They smiled and admired him, all while embracing each other.

"Wow," he thought, as the vision faded. "That's me as an infant." He needed to reaffirm the obvious for it to fully register in his mind.

The scene transitioned to him as an adolescent. He watched, from a third person perspective, sitting with his parents at their sacred table. It was when his parents found out that he snuck through the forcefield fence and ventured out of the valley. He had been gone a long time, and when they questioned him, Sozwik admitted that he had slipped out of the valley.

This was dangerous business, as no Jyoti had left the valley since the enslavement. The Guard kept vigilant watch, so no one dared to even venture near the forcefield for fear of the consequences. Though at the time it seemed like they were angry, he could now see it was a mixture of worry and pride. They never asked exactly how he did it and it was never spoken of after that, but they always kept it in the back of their minds.

Anda and Macha were well-learned in Wakanry themselves. And though they were concerned for his safety, they could foresee him as an agent of change for their race. Sozwik was hyper-sensitive to the unseen and his intense curiosity often outmatched his fears. For these very reasons, Sozwik's parents had carefully chosen Goa to be his teacher.

Looking back, Sozwik embraced a reinvigorated gratitude for his parents. He reached out through the ethers and bid them another heartfelt goodbye as they were peacefully in their dream states.

"I know they always have my back. I'm taken care of." A feeling of loving reassurance vibrated through him and brought his consciousness back into his body.

Ω

Then, finding himself standing amongst the dark, tranquil shadows of vegetation, Sozwik felt as if he were floating in an ocean of deep peace. In this state, he wholly surrendered to his situation and vowed to make the most of it. "It is what it is. And embrace it I shall," Sozwik thought to himself.

Chapter 3
Welcome to Earth

It was like snapping into a dream...

The blue-white light faded. Sozwik found himself standing amidst dense wilderness, in a moment of absolute stillness.

Then suddenly a tidal wave of sensory input surged through his being. The lush forest, the chirping of birds, the brisk breeze, the intuitive chatter of countless beings, the deep, blue sky, the feeling of grass on his feet; it was all so mesmerizing. He couldn't help but brandish a blissful grin.

It was eerily similar to Seren, yet so alien at the same time. The general themes of the vegetation and landscapes were closely resemblant. Yet in taking a closer look, Sozwik saw the distinctness. There were trees and plants he had never seen before, in shapes and colors that stretched his sense of possibility. And, of course, the ebbing and flowing of the landscape is always unique to each place, regardless of the planet one is on.

Sozwik looked at a mountain in the distance and it came to life. Her massive base commanded respect. Her ascending green body, dotted with light-brown cliffs, gave off a merry warmth. And her snow-capped summit smiled like a mother greeting her son. Light radiated over the mountain like a halo, beautifully completing her awesome, alluring aura.

The only thing the Jyoti loved more than a well-made treehouse was a beautiful landscape. By having what seemed like unlimited access to the vast territory of Earth, all thoughts of the past and future disappeared (for now). Sozwik's curiosity overran his fears. His whole being erupted with excitement.

It was clear where he had to go. And he almost had no choice in the matter.

His feet set him in motion. Instinct took over as Sozwik deftly meandered through the underbrush, sliding through the thick forest as he'd done his entire life on Seren.

In an explosion of leaves and sticks, like he was being rebirthed by Mother Nature, Sozwik burst out of the thicket into an open boulder field. Massive stony structures towered above as he moved through, climbing, ducking, and winding.

It opened up to a precipitous, rocky section that sat proudly above the tree line. The steep section was glossed with sheets of snow. Not fazed by elemental curveballs, Sozwik dropped his hands to the ground in mid-stride. His two-legged gait effortlessly transitioned into a four-legged, uphill crawl. Sozwik's massive shoulders flexed through his hair as his powerful arms propelled him up, which immediately morphed into a slight squat and a launch from his robust legs. This dynamic hand-walking cycle was repeated so fast that snow was kicked up in his wake, like an avalanche thundering upward.

Sozwik rapidly approached a thick barrier of jagged rocks that stood between him and the summit. In a dance of breakneck brachiation, he swung swiftly through crevices and quickly climbed the craggy constructs.

He came out of the jagged jungle into a surreal alpine field. It was almost completely flat, and covered in short, stocky grass. From here, Sozwik could see the zenith of the mountain.

He needed to reach that peak. It was calling him. One of those subtle hints of communication that inanimate objects (well, inanimate by human standards) often emit.

Breaking into a two-legged gallop, Sozwik made his way up the final slope. Rock-hopping and skipping uphill as if gravity were only a force of belief, he rounded the bald crown of the majestic mountain.

360-degree views of serene, green forestry flooded into Sozwik's conscious awareness. "This has to be the climax of worldly landscapes," he thought to himself.

Sozwik was at her peak, overlooking a new reality. The connection with the towering mountain instilled within him profound appreciation of everything he saw. The ridgelines looked like the spines of giant creatures. The trees were like the cells of a superorganism. The luscious Earth seamlessly kissed the sky at the horizon.

Sozwik flashed back to that occasion on Seren where he was able to sneak out of the valley, through a secret tunnel underneath the forcefield fence, and roam the mountain ranges. That feeling of profound awe came back to him as he continued to gaze out at the landscape.

When the sense of wonder wandered away, his thoughts drew back to Seren. "It would give me comfort," Sozwik thought, "To just know that I'm ever connected to my kin on Seren."

Sozwik closed his eyes and attempted to reach out through the ethers, but there was nothing… Radio silence. It was as if there was a subtle and undetectable block. "I'll try again later," Sozwik muttered, compromising with himself.

There was nothing he could do now. The sense of urgency turned into helplessness and helplessness turned into acceptance. "And so it is."

Ω

"Since I can't communicate, I might as well physically survey where I am," Sozwik reasoned, almost to convince himself.

With nothing else to do, Sozwik swept his worry aside spent some time on the mountain and its neighboring peaks. He immersed himself in the environment and allowed the fluid wisdom of nature to guide him. Once he fully entered this state of flow, worlds of possibilities opened to him.

Sozwik was absolutely overcome with urges of intense, childlike exploration. He gallivanted around the hulking cliffs, ran through the streams and climbed the gargantuan trees. Running full speed across the landscapes, it felt as if his feet were actually moving the ground beneath him. Hills rolled under his steps with the bittersweet hello-goodbye of quick-lived but profound relationships.

It is said that movement through forestry brings a Jyoti closer to his or her essence. Sozwik did just that. He ran as close to the essence as reality would allow, like an asymptote on a graph moving ever closer to the axis yet never being absolutely there.

Soon the novelty of the new planet gave way to the scope of the situation at hand. Sozwik also had a lingering feeling of loneliness that he didn't know how to deal with. He had never spent more than a day by his lonesome. And he had never been completely out of contact with those he cared for. Both were true now, and it triggered a torrent of mental disquiet.

Questions flooded Sozwik's brain. Too many for any specific ones to even register. Then a dizzying storm of mental babbling came over him.

"What if I can never communicate with anyone ever again? Let alone see my kin in the flesh. And I can't just frolic forever while so much is going on. Well, I can, but I know I shouldn't. Ugh, not even shouldn't. I just know I have more to offer. I have to do something. But what? I don't even have a clue where I am (besides being on Earth)."

Playful ignorance could be fun, but Sozwik knew that gaily running around the remote woods of Earth wouldn't be fulfilling for long. "The Guard's tracking me. It thinks I'm as mind-controlled as they come. Ha! I need to collect more information on The Guard. Also, about humans and my kin on Seren. Plus, I have a sneaking suspicion that there's a greater purpose yet to be revealed."

Sozwik felt fatigue creeping up, poised to pounce upon him and drag him into the dreamscapes of sleep. Time may be just a concept, but interplanetary jet lag is felt by all mortal beings.

In a humble cave he had stumbled upon, Sozwik assembled his sleeping quarters. It was a pleasant dwelling, immune to the elements. For his bed, Sozwik used a collection of leaves, which he condensed, with his tremendous hand strength, into a suitable mattress to lay upon. It was no treehouse, but it worked out just fine.

Then it was time to illuminate the cave with the gift of the fire element. First was his search for something to start the fire, the sacrificial objects of flame inauguration. His hands worked adeptly together to gather tinder for forging the fire. Sozwik snapped large branches off of dead trees and arranged them in a teepee-like structure.

Sozwik then started the fire with an ancient Jyoti technique. It was a technique wholly dependent on the Jyoti's immensely explosive power. Sozwik held a small, but sturdy stick. In a flash of primal dynamism, Sozwik swept the stick down, running it along the floor of the cave to produce a blazing line. At the end of this line was a small pile of dry leaves, which received the spark well. Sozwik's first fire on Earth was in progress.

In the dim, red light of the fire, Sozwik partook in a ritual meditation. He crossed his right leg over his left leg and slowly lowered himself until he was seated on the ground. Sozwik entered the spiritual realms through the gateway of his breath. It began with deep, long inhales through his prominent nostrils, followed by a sacred pause, then long exhales. Sozwik inhaled serenity and exhaled fear until he was watching his mind from a bird's eye view. His thoughts played like a movie on a screen.

From here, Sozwik was able to muse about the concept of time. In order to better adjust to Earth, it would be important to be more cognizant of "Earth time." In the theatre of his mind, Sozwik replayed a teaching Goa had relayed to him regarding the slippery notion of time…

Ω

"Sozwik, there is a pertinent piece of information to discuss before your journey to Earth. And that is the concept of time.

Our Jyoti concept of time is similar to some ancient civilizations on Earth. In fact, the ways of the Jyoti were in fact the basis of the great ancient cultures of Earth, but that's a long, complex tale itself with many middlemen involved.

Human time is thought of as something linear, while we Jyoti view time as a cyclical spiral, mimicking the movements of celestial bodies. You may not be able to fathom this, Sozwik, as "Jyoti time" is all you know.

Let's use Seren as an example. Seren revolves around The Great Star, its sun. But the system itself is not stationary (well, nothing is) because The Great Star's entire system is revolving around the center of its galaxy, the Pleo galaxy (which is an elliptical galaxy, different than Earth's Milky Way galaxy, which is a spiral galaxy). If one was to map out the path of Seren, it would not be a circle, but a spiral, moving in a cyclical pattern yet always in a different place.

This, in our Jyoti view, is how time moves as well, because time is essentially a measure of movement. Since everything moves in spiraling cycles, it only makes sense for time to be laid out in spiraling cycles as well. Everything in existence goes through cycles, but these cycles are always slightly different. A Jyoti's life can be measured in the cycles of light and dark, but at the end of each cycle, the Jyoti has more experience and is (hopefully) wiser. The life cycle of a Jyoti is akin to the life cycle of civilizations, which is akin to the life cycle of planets, which is akin to the life cycle of stars, which is akin to the life cycle of galaxies, and so on and so forth. As above, so below. As below, so above.

Having a system of spiral-time creates harmony between the concept of time and the movement it attempts to measure. Placing a linear template upon the spiraling movements of celestial bodies (like most humans do) creates a foundation of disharmony. This time-space disharmony, along with being trapped in the egoic self (due to a cunning bait and switch tactic by The Guard), is what creates an underlying feeling of fear regarding time. The past is looked at with regret, or hopelessly longed for again, while the future is met with anxiety or projected excitement. In both cases, the present moment is missed.

The Jyoti belief is that the past, present and future all exist in the "Eternal Now." When viewed from a higher dimension, three-dimensional reality is quite like what humans call a video game (which is essentially a simulated life). The past, present and future (along with all possibilities) are encoded within the video game. It all exists simultaneously on a higher dimension, and incarnating into physical reality is merely focusing your point of attention within a "level" of the game. This point of attention is what us humans call the present moment that we experience. But outside of this niche viewpoint, all exists simultaneously.

Us Jyoti — as you know, Sozwik — accept the past and future as a part of the Eternal Now. The past is the momentum carried into the present and the future is where you're going. In our tradition of Wakanry, the present moment is referred to as "the ever-moving point of unending actualization which encases the physical dimension." It is the point of power which physical beings travel in that creates the future and changes one's relationship with the past.

Remember the sailing ship metaphor that we were all given as children? The past is the wake, and the future is where you're headed. You can see how you came to be by observing the wake, and where you're going by which direction the ship is pointed. But the present moment is the steering. One cannot change the past by jumping into the wake or alter the future by jumping in front of the ship. All actions occur, have occurred, and always will occur, through the ship's steering wheel. Through the steering of the present moment, you can change both your relationship with the wake behind you (past) and the direction in which you're going (future).

This is why we are hyper-aware of when we're marinating on the past or future. We acutely feel emotions like anxiety, a fear-gap between the present and future, and proactively rid ourselves of it upon its provocation. We place great emphasis on residing in the present moment and cherishing it, because it's the only place where we can influence the Eternal Now. Of course, we refer to the past to learn from it, and look to the future when planning, but this is all done in the present moment, and it all exists in the Eternal Now.

The present moment is also the "access point" to the Eternal Now. You're very familiar with this, Sozwik, but it's important to repeat. The deeper you immerse yourself in the moment, the more the progression of time slows down. It slows and slows and slows until you've completely unclenched the grip of time and drift into the Eternal Now, where time as we know it ceases to be a part of your experience. After the enslavement, most Jyoti lost the ability to reach this state, but it is a core aspect of Wakanry that you and I are torch bearers of.

Measuring time in spiraling cycles is incredibly difficult for the human mind to grasp, just as it's incredibly difficult for us to only think linearly.

We view time as a winding spiral, like that of the Phi spiral, as opposed to the time-LINES that most humans on Earth use. While most humans use a base 10 numerical system, we use a base 12 numerical system, which is a far more accurate template to place upon observable phenomena.

Conversions can be made between Jyoti and human constructs of time. Though not entirely accurate, they help bridge the gap between paradigms of understanding. Human measurements of days, months and years all have their Jyoti equivalents (which are slightly different but far more precise). A Jyoti day, a cycle of light and dark or a rotation of Seren, is the equivalent of approximately 51.4 Earth hours. A Jyoti year, a revolution of Seren around The Great Star, is the equivalent of approximately 10 Earth years. Factoring in the difference in time measurement, the variation in planetary movement, the Jyoti body's incredible robustness and the fact that Seren's solar system was in a fast-moving section of its galaxy, most Jyoti would live the equivalent of about 1,000 Earth years. This is good news for you, Sozwik, as you'll be able to observe a lot of change take place on Earth.

Also, our paradigm of time is why Jyoti stories are told in spiraling fashion. And rumor has it that human stories are told in linear fashion. That is hard to grasp, but you may come to understand it more during your time on Earth, Sozwik. Just tune into the moment and let your intuition guide the way. Rules are meant to be broken, yet must not be done carelessly."

Ω

Sozwik meditated on Goa's insights. He wondered if being on Earth would cause his memory to be slowly stretched, or flattened, from a spiral to a more linear phenomenon. This was a lot to grok and would take a while to fully realize.

After cycling through these remembrances and musings, Sozwik let the lingering thoughts fade and connected with the whole. No longer within the confinements of place and time, he steeped his being in the blissful nectar of infinity.

Chapter 4
Meanwhile on Seren

Back on Seren, Goa was trudging through the troubles of his own mind.

Even he was not immune to the perils of the mind, for he had one just like everyone else.

The Wakan view is that the mind will always find problems. And it's in transcending the mind that you can use it as a tool without being consumed by its problem-finding (or problem-creating) ways.

This generation of freed Jyoti had just departed, and Goa could feel an ever-increasing sense of urgency through the ethers. Combine this with what he had gleaned from Paupo, the eldest of the Jyoti on Earth, in the vision-space, and Goa was understandably restless.

Goa was one of the few who had more than a mere sliver of understanding of the expansive breadth of the interplanetary scenario at hand. But even he felt the frustrating paralysis of ignorance now, which can be tormenting for any knowledge seeker.

Goa sat in the center of his isolated treehouse in deep meditation. With everything going on, and Sozwik (who he had grown very fond of over the years) leaving, a "spring cleaning of the mind" was necessary. Goa went through all the nooks and crannies of his psyche and cleared out all of the doubts, fear, worry, anxiety, regret and the like. It was of no use carrying these things. They would only hinder his ability to help.

Finding peace as the waters of his mind stilled, Goa reassured himself: "My role lies here on Seren."

Ω

Goa was known to be the eldest Jyoti on Seren, and certainly the most maverick of the species at this point.

No one knew his actual age, and it mattered little to him. He seemed to stand in defiance to the aging process, much like he did with everything else. He was viewed as an enigma of almost mythical proportions. Many Jyoti joked about his apparent agelessness, as he still looked and acted like a Jyoti in his prime. A favorite hyperbolic saying among the Jyoti was, "Goa kicked the ground once, and Seren has been spinning around The Great Star ever since."

Goa was born in the first generation of slavery and was the only living Jyoti on Seren to have lived among the free ancestors. Because of this, Goa was thoroughly schooled in the mystical Wakan ways by the formerly free elders of the race. In other words, Goa was a cultural bridge. He walked between worlds, tiptoeing between the metaphysical effervescence of the free ancestors and the programmed reality of the present enslavement era.

Those elders, who had lived most of their lives in freedom, seemed almost a different species. Though still grounded in kindness, they were less inclined to kowtow to The Guard's orders. They retained a sense of pride and healthy rebelliousness that the preceding generations who grew up in enslavement seemed to lack.

This rebellious, free spirit got most of these Jyoti killed in the first years of enslavement. There were many organized non-compliance movements in those days. The main form of protest was simply refusing to work at the mines and standing outside taunting The Guard. But the Jyoti had not realized the full scope of The Guard's dubiosity. There was no empathy, which the jovial Jyoti could hardly fathom. So, in true fashion, The Guard just mercilessly annihilated all protesters until all the most daring were either dead or had their spirits beaten into subservience.

Goa himself had almost gotten killed several times when he was younger and more reckless.

The Jyoti are highly intelligent though, especially when it comes to The Big Picture. The few that were left realized that it was more important to furtively pass on their esoteric secrets to the younger generations as opposed to openly challenging The Guard. For the ways of the Jyoti, particularly the Wakan tradition, were far beyond the greedy reach of The Guard.

The metaphorical "Jyoti Tree" (the term they used to describe the culmination of their culture) was demolished. But within the consciousness of those formerly free Jyoti laid the seeds for a new, possibly more robust, tree.

All Jyoti had much knowledge that The Guard was utterly oblivious to, and Goa was the prime example.

Every Jyoti, male and female worked in the zapixion mines from the age of seven until death. Before the age of seven was their "schooling."

Goa, being as clever and mischievous as a nycono, had faked his own death and was now living out the rest of his life in "retirement" under The Guard's radar. This "rebirthed retirement" eventually became the precedent for elders fluent in Wakanry. There weren't many left, and they were desperately needed to keep those esoteric ways alive.

Goa devoted most of his time to further developing his own abilities and secretly training others in Wakanry. Sozwik was his latest apprentice.

Ω

With the refreshment of meditation reverberating through his being, Goa decided to pay Sozwik's parents a visit that night, after everyone was released from the mines.

He had known both of them since they were children and all three had always gotten along well. In the Jyoti community, each child has their parents, yet the whole community plays as the role of third parent. The villages were tight-knit, and everyone helped each other out.

The old saying was, "A net of 1,000 ropes is reliable to fall back on. But a net made of just a few will either break or you'll slip through."

Much of the Jyoti ways were compromised due to the enslavement, but still some of their culture was steadfastly preserved, for they knew that any hope of throwing The Guard off their back depended on it.

Walking up to Anda and Macha's treehouse with his famous swagger, Goa let out a Wakan greeting call. To the untrained ear, it would've sounded something like a laughing bird.

The ominous feeling of the times at hand was still ever-present, but Goa now felt more clear-headed and sought to illuminate the darkness.

The moment his call was answered, Goa launched himself upward, grabbed a branch and propelled his body his body into a front-flip, landing in between Anda and Macha on their elevated porch.

"You still got it going on," said Macha with a childlike laugh.

"A bit of play clears the troubles away," replied Goa, smirking back at him.

Macha and Anda together embraced Goa and their lighthearted greeting swiftly sank into the depths of their intense emotions.

"Have you heard from Sozwik?" asked Anda. "We've been reaching out and haven't even felt a trace of him."

"The same with me," replied Goa, slowly bowing his head down.

"I knew that communication is supposed to be very limited on Earth, but I'm not totally ignorant," said Macha, disarming his joking self for a moment. His face turned more serious. "I know the most adept Wakans can communicate with those on Earth, and it's kept secret. I expected at least some exchange with Sozzy."

"This is true," replied Goa. "Some things must be nurtured only in the safest wombs before being revealed to all." Goa let it sink in before continuing. "The fact that there's no real signal could mean many things. Maybe, together we can reach through the ethers and see if the collective energy makes a difference."

Eagerly obliging, Anda and Macha formed a triangle around Goa and all three went into meditation, deeply breathing and slowly transcending the busyness of their minds.

The group seemed to pierce a veil and they felt Sozwik's presence. What were usually clear emotions now felt like phantoms of feelings. Everything seemed so distant.

Drawing their energy closer, all they heard was broken whispers of Sozwik's thoughts…

"What was that sound?"

"A human!"

"Does he see me?"

A feeling of alarm swept over them, and they were shaken out of their meditative state. Goa's eyes opened to see Macha and Anda looking at each other, faces heavily painted with concern.

The faint murmurs they heard were troubling. They feared for Sozwik's safety.

To calm their energy, Goa spoke. "Yes, that was unclear and ominous. But what can we do from here? I have much faith in Sozwik."

Anda's voice melodiously carried through the room. "We have faith in him too, though it's frightful to tune into something so vague and augural. Still, we fear for our son's safety."

"Let's check into the vision-space," recommended Goa.

Each species has what the Jyoti call a "vision-space." These are realms, of sorts, with unique frequencies for each species. The home planet of the species acts as a projector point for the vision-space, so when beings are "tuned in" to the planet they're on, they can effectively access and communicate through this space.

Easing their way out of the clutches on anxiety, Goa, Anda and Macha tuned into the Jyoti's vision-space.

Their spirits were deflated yet again. No one was there.

They slowly brought their consciousness back into the room. For the rest of the night, they talked, each expressing their concern and brainstorming solutions. In the end, Goa decided that he would call for a council meeting. The Guard's influence was accelerating, and time was of the essence.

Anda and Macha were at least partially renewed with some hope when Goa left their treehouse in the depths of night.

"The window of both danger and opportunity opens," Goa said to himself as he wound through the trees back to his own abode.

Ω

The next morning, Goa sent out a call for a council meeting.

The Jyoti had no official form of government. Day-to-day business was handled in a cooperative, free-flowing, egalitarian manner. Every Jyoti was the master of themselves, and each acted in the best interest of the village, for they viewed themselves as individual cells in the same body. With that perspective, it was to the benefit of all to keep the collective healthy. Though this paradigm was shaking a little bit due to The Guard's programming, it still held strong as the undercurrent of Jyoti culture.

Major decisions, however, were treated a bit differently. All major decisions were made by a council of 12 elder women who were both wise and thoroughly proficient in Wakanry. Women were the major decision-makers for the simple fact that men of any species tend to be more inclined to violence and war. This informal maternal council had kept the Jyoti in peace and harmony since their genesis, which was incredibly rare for any species in this dimension.

Secondly, the elder women knew all of the Jyoti men since birth and played a role in raising all of them. Every council member was viewed as a grandmother figure, even by the most ambitious and headstrong male, and their opinions were greatly respected.

And thirdly (among many more reasons), the intuition cultivated by elder women was seen to be in seamless congruency with The Big Picture. In having a council of elder women to make necessary decisions, the Jyoti would be in harmony with the Universe as a whole.

The decisions of the council were also agreed upon by the rest of the elders afterward, and then accepted by each individual of the village. Because of the loving congruency of the elder women with the Big Picture, this set-up was in perpetual harmony with the highest good of the village. Not once in their Ourstory (The Jyoti translation of "history") did a council attempt to exhibit control over the tribe. The Jyoti had developed such a level of self-mastery, synergy and abundance that the desire to control others was laughable from their paradigm.

Since the enslavement began, these councils operated in secrecy because The Guard did not allow meeting of more than 10 Jyoti unless it was an approved event. It was also never in a fixed location to further avoid detection.

Since Goa sent out the call, the council meeting took place in his own home. Goa was standing, pondering all-too-much when the dozen council members whistled their secret password from outside, only to appear all around him by the time the beautiful, bird-like sound ended.

"It was a wise decision to call the council, Goa," said Dara, a highly respected councilmember who just so happened to be the daughter of Goa's brother. "Many of us have felt the song of the universe coming to a crescendo, especially since the freeing yesterday."

Relieved to have the support of others, Goa confessed, "I am growing troubled."

"That's why we shall talk," replied Dara with the compassion only a wisened elder was capable of exuding.

Goa and the council members all sat in a circle, and everyone gave their own input on the situation and expressed their hopes and fears. He then explained his glimpse into Sozwik's thoughts…

"Sozwik is in some sort of danger. What it is exactly, I do not know. Anda, Macha and I reached through the ethers, and we heard faded pieces of Sozwik's thoughts. This is all we heard:

'What was that sound?'
'A human!'
'Does he see me?'

And then his voice cut off as quickly as it appeared."

"It's troubling to hear and he may have gotten to close to humans. And I hope The Guard was not tracking him too closely when this happened," said Dara.

"His curiosity may have finally gotten the best of him," quipped another council member in a skeptical tone.

Though some scoffed at his rebellious spirit, the council generally liked Sozwik, though none knew him quite as well as Goa of course, who spoke again.

"I'll tell you all this, as this is my premonition. Sozwik, like it or not, has become the harbinger of action. What I mean by this is that the fate of our species is dangles by a fine thread. We can no longer sit around in this valley, acquiescing to our own slavery! Action must be taken unless we wish to be driven into the darkest age the Jyoti have ever known and enslaved indefinitely beyond hope of freedom!"

"I agree," replied Dara. "But we must not act in haste. How are we to reverse this predicament so quickly?"

Goa answered… "We need to glean as much knowledge as possible. We must act as antennas, picking up any and every useful signal we can. We need a complete briefing of all Jyoti on Earth who are in communication and as much information regarding The Guard as we can possibly gather. And we must do this as soon as Jyoti-ly possible. The solution will present itself in this process."

"What's so frustrating about The Guard is that so much is kept hidden," said Olea, one of the council members. "But we do know ourselves, so that's as good of a start as any."

She continued by saying, "My dear friend Fala and I will frequent the vision-space as often as we can and act as liaisons for the Earth-bound Jyoti. We will have to sacrifice some duties here on Seren and need some cover, so The Guard doesn't catch on to our activities."

"We can cover you," said Dara reassuringly.

All of those present also knew that there was an urgent need for more Jyoti who were well-versed in Wakanry. It was also agreed that each elder would take on five young Jyoti to train them in the Wakan ways, in addition to whoever they were currently training.

Dara spoke what was on everyone's mind…

"In such turbulent times, we need as many wisened individuals as possible. It's worth the risk of The Guard finding out because the alternative is our species slipping further into the darkness of slavery."

They reached out through the ethers and asked the rest of the elders if they agreed with this notion and the response was a unanimous "yes."

Each elder was designated five young Jyoti who showed Wakan potential and the meeting, as per usual, was ended with song and a group hug.

Ω

Goa was to teach Abeo, Bena, Zaltana, Kuwa and Wogo.

Though this was exciting for him, he would be able to access the vision-space far less frequently than he had before, as training would be the top priority.

Instilling the Wakan wisdom within willing Jyoti was Goa's expertise. Almost every Jyoti on Seren who was well-versed in Wakanry could credit their skills to Goa.

Now, more than ever, it was crucial to keep this momentum in motion.

It seemed to Goa that each generation of young Jyoti was more lost than the last. The programming was compounding through each successive generation.

All the elders began teaching their respective students immediately, starting the night of the council meeting. "Operation Wakan 101" as Goa like to call it, was underway. Yet he feared that this last-ditch effort might have been too late, but either way they had no choice but to give it their all. The fate of the Jyoti hung in a fine balance.

Out of Goa's group, only Wogo was able to even observe his own thoughts with regularity. This is only because he was Paupo's great grandson, and that family was one of the few (like Sozwik's family) who proactively preserved the ways of Wakanry.

With the other four, Goa could sense the cloud of programming immediately. It would be much work, even though all his pupils were very young.

Based upon the consciousness-inhibiting effects of programming on his students, Goa's teaching would be in three phases. Firstly, enough Wakan wisdom must be cultivated for the individual to deprogram, then the process of deprogramming would take place, and finally the true learning of Wakanry. It would be an intensive crash course, but desperate times often push beings beyond previous bounds of possibility.

Goa met with his group every evening, for the race of tipping points was on.

Chapter 5
The Hunter

A powerful *"CRACK"* in the distance snapped Sozwik out of his trance.

Icy chills of terror penetrated his whole body. Primal fear reverberated up his spine, shook up his neck and opened his eyes with anxious vigilance.

The Top Rank were known for being proudly (and even stubbornly) stoic, but Sozwik was on a foreign planet and stirred to his core.

His mind scanned its database of relatable references for an answer. The sound was somewhere between the snap of a thick branch and the blast of The Guards' laser guns. Whatever it was, Sozwik knew that he had to be on his toes.

He rose to his feet and crept out of the cave with curious caution. The first rays of sunlight were making their way over the landscape, giving the environment a surreal, dreamlike quality. Long shadows of trees stretched over everything, the grasses were glazed with dew and peculiar birds sang songs celebrating dawn.

With intense alertness, Sozwik made his way towards the source of the astonishing sound. He maneuvered like a shark, fluidly swimming in silence through the dense underbrush.

"CRACK!" The sound pierced his ears. This time it was uncomfortably close. Sozwik tip-toed his way towards a clearing to get a good view. He hid behind a gargantuan tree and slowly leaned his head out like a scout on the lookout.

Movement… Just on the other side of the clearing. Before he could make out the specific features, Sozwik knew it was a human. The human was adorned in clothing that blended with the environment almost perfectly. Though its body seemed to be hairless, its head and face had some hair. Most peculiar of all, the way it crept through the woods was much slower and awkward than even the least agile Jyoti. Sozwik almost laughed, but then he saw it… The human raised what looked like a primitive version of the guards' laser rifles. And it pointed directly at him.

They stared at each other for what seemed like an eternity. Sozwik, letting his fear fall at the feet of this intrinsic connection, reached out through the unseen realms to try to communicate with the human. The first thing he noticed was that the human was utterly terrified, maybe even more so than himself. Sozwik emitted energetic thought-forms of compassion and kinship towards the human. And as they mingled with his field, he felt the human begin to reciprocate the same energy.

Time stood still.

For this mini-eternity, Sozwik understood. It was total understanding. He truly knew this human and all humans in a way that his mind couldn't quite grasp. But as he reached for an explanation, he slipped back through the fabric of space and time.

The universe spun back into motion as the human lowered his clumsy version of a laser rifle. The human shook his head in disbelief, as if to wake himself from a dream, then turned around and ran in the opposite direction.

Sozwik chose to not follow the peculiar being.

The Guard's strict orders played out in an ominous loop in his head… "You are free to roam the wilderness of Planet Earth. Do not interfere with human affairs and do not let humans even see you."

His thoughts then moved to the Top Rank Badge which gripped his right ankle like a parasitic snake.

"And this thing…" Sozwik growled in frustration, wishing it wasn't there.

One of Goa's favorite old Wakan poems came to him…

"I have eyes to see the situations I can't control
I have eyes to see those I can
Yet no matter the matter
I always hold the power
To control my own reactions"

Realizing that he could do nothing about the tracking device right now, he closed his eyes and breathed away his frustrations.

Sozwik still stood motionless, in the same spot where he had seen the human, and pondered his situation.

The human seemed so out of place in the forest. "A stark contrast to the Jyoti," he thought. Sozwik wondered that perhaps humans are unsuited for their own planet and ineffective out of their urban establishments. Well, it was common knowledge that they were contained within their communities for the most part.

"But why?" Sozwik pondered as the parachute of his musings landed him in the jungle of inquisitive nature…

"Are humans a cousin to us Jyoti? It surely felt as such."
"What happened to their hair?"
"What was this human doing?"
"Why do humans seem incompetent in their own habitat?"
"Is this really their habitat?"
"Where are these grand cities that have been rumored to exist?"

"Does The Guard allow humans to roam freely?"

"And where are my fellow Jyoti?"

These questions circled in Sozwik's curious mind, like birds of prey spiraling high above an open field, eagerly searching for any trace of movement unfathomably far below. Yet he knew that it would take the patience of a great, wise bird to allow the answers to reveal themselves.

Sozwik then felt guilt begin to bubble up in his consciousness. "Had I slipped up and came too close to one of the more maverick humans?" The feeling grew into a strange brew of guilt mixed with a vague longing for connection with the human he had seen. Sozwik felt as if he shared the same inconceivably distant genesis with the man. Acknowledging the feeling fully, he then centered himself back into the present moment.

Sozwik gazed out at the field of the encounter and gave it a tributary nod.

He slowly moved his hands to the center of his chest and began tapping, slowly transmuting the fear stirred up by the encounter back into harmony.

Chapter 6

Where are All of the Humans?

Sozwik's feet gently urged him back into motion as the last shreds of shock slowly wilted away.

"That human must have been more scared than I was." He laughed to himself, in an attempt to lure his courage back, like how you and I would call for an untamed dog that ran away. But courage, like a dog that isn't quite domesticated, comes back when you least expect it.

Fear soon faded in favor of the spirit of exploration, and on he went.

Hopping over a fallen tree, Sozwik made his way up a steep slope. Once he gained elevation, he turned and looked at the scenery behind him. The pristine wilderness spanned as far as the eye can see. Sozwik wondered where these human settlements could be. Were they so small and isolated? Because in this area, all he came across was thick forest.

Sozwik ran up and along the precipitous rail of a ridgeline, revering the rolling green hills. The speed was thrilling, and combined with the open views, left Sozwik feeling brilliantly alive.

Ω

Sozwik stopped to rest. The pause of activity made him aware of the hunger arising within. His body called for sustenance, something replenishing.

Some of the great Jyoti ancestors, through long years of Wakan training, learned to absorb and convert the light of The Great Star for sustenance. But Sozwik wasn't there yet. Plus, he loved the taste, the sensory pleasure, of physical food and wasn't yet ready to give that up. Goa once told him that he (Goa) had learned to sustain himself through "Jyotisynthesis" (his term for converting light into sustenance) but chose not to because he loved the taste of food too much. "Maybe next lifetime," Goa laughed when he and Sozwik once discussed the matter.

The Jyoti didn't place living beings in a hierarchy. Plants and animals were all celebrated as unique, yet equals. Everything was revered as sacred and all were treated with respect, especially when giving their life as food. With this being said, the Jyoti generally did not eat animals. It was unnecessary on Seren, which boasted an abundance of easily accessible plant matter to fill the Jyoti's physical needs. Plus, the only other sizable animal in the valley were nyconos, which were as hard to catch as one's own shadow.

Sozwik shifted his consciousness into his nose. He focused until he literally became the rhythmic inhale and exhale. Then his being was flooded with a redolent, slightly sweet smell. Sozwik connected with what he sensed to be plant-matter containing dense nutrition. His nose was the receiver of a multi-dimensional transmission, and as he followed the frequency path, it became stronger and stronger. Both the connection and the smell reached a crescendo as he came upon a dense conglomeration of short bushes, glowing with a vibrant blue gleam. Sozwik slowly stepped to the closest one. He held out his hand and touched the blue, spherical object that had called to him. Sozwik bowed his head in reverence to the generous spirit behind this plant, for it was both friendly and helpful. Then he gently pulled it off of its home and placed it upon his forehead.

The Communiverse instantly opened…

"Greetings friend," said the jovial sphere of a blue plant.

"Hello," Sozwik replied. It was more like an exchange of feelings than actual words. But Sozwik had done this with some of the more amicable plants on Seren as well, so he already had basic fluency, enough to translate energy-speak into words. Still, it was surprising to him, especially since he had no idea of what this plant was.

The plant went on. "You can call me Blueberry. My kind sustains many of the large creatures of this region. We're glad to be of service."

"Thank you," Sozwik replied.

The plant continued. And Sozwik was happy, yet he didn't know what to say. He felt like a young Jyoti again, tongue-tied when trying to talk to the pretty Ti-fees (slang for young Jyoti females).

"So, what are you looking for? Besides sustenance," said Blueberry in a playful tone.

"I don't know." Sozwik felt vulnerable and surprised that the plant could feel that he was searching for something he didn't quite understand.

"Open up communication with your kind. They've been around awhile. Very thoughtful and kind-hearted creatures the Jyoti are. You might find out more from them."

"Yes, I shall do that," said Sozwik.

"Humans, The Guard, slavery and freedom, it's all a game. Don't be afraid to let everything run its course, Sozwik. But sometimes running its course means doing something to allow existence to run its course."

Sozwik hesitated. "I don't understand."

"You soon will. Now get on with it and let's assimilate into that vessel of yours. You're hungry and my friends and I are ready for some new adventures."

"Ok. Yes, yes," muttered Sozwik with bashful reverence. "Thank you." Sozwik then removed Blueberry from his forehead and held it in front of his face.

A humming prayer emanated from the depths of his soul, enveloping the two beings in a cocoon of gratitude. The humming tailed off as Sozwik passed Blueberry through his lips.

Its texture was sturdy yet yielding, not slippery yet not rough. Sozwik slowly bit down, and sweet juice seeped out. A tinge of sourness complemented the candied taste, creating a swirl of succulent flavor. As Sozwik chewed the fleshy inside, the full bliss of the smell reached his nose. A deep inhale brought Sozwik into an intense state of gratitude. He opened his eyes and smiled at the life-giving qualities of nature.

Sozwik, in pure delight, ate many more of the blueberry friends, stopping when his body finally gave the signal of satiety.

Basking in the fulfillment of both needs and pleasure, Sozwik laid down in the hidden middle of the blueberry patch.

Lying back-to-back with the Earth, he could almost feel her breathing, just as he was. She comforted him, grounding his energy and relieving any sense of loss he harbored since his departure from Seren. Sozwik also gave his anxieties of the future to Earth. As he did, the Earth itself replied with a message. "Stay grounded in me, you already have all of the answers you seek." He sighed in relief.

After some time, Sozwik rose to his feet and decided it was time to continue his journey.

Ω

Moving like a silent breeze, Sozwik listened to the sound of wind running through the leaves of trees. The gentle rattle reverberated through his ears like an auditory massage.

He stopped and hopped on a pronounced rock. The protruding, nose-shaped structure beckoned him to stand upon it. From this small perch, Sozwik took it all in. Slowly spinning, he admired the panoramic view with a smile. It was an undulation of deep green in every direction, kissed by the blue sky gleefully reaching down upon the Earth.

Dusk was slowly rolling upon the land. The mysterious aura of twilight brought the trees to life, like lumbering whimsical giants that seemed to be waving at the world.

Sozwik gazed at the amalgamation of shadows on display in the forest below. "It's all a game of shadows," Sozwik thought to himself. "Day and night are a tide of shadows, as am I, as is life."

Reflecting upon this insight, Sozwik closed his eyes and completely immersed himself in the moment. Oh, the beauty of it.

A gentle breeze stroked Sozwik's cheek, coaxing him to open his eyes.

It felt so good; a feeling of ecstasy bubbled up to the point where it was uncontainable. In a fit of joy, Sozwik front-flipped off the rock and hit the ground skipping. Artful lunges brought him downhill like the antlered, four-legged creatures of the woods he had spotted several times.

Happily testing his vessel, Sozwik jumped up, snapping a branch high on a tree. The Jyoti tended to do this out of excitement.

Flashing back to his favorite game of Downhill, Sozwik leapt over fallen trees and speedily tightroped over long roots. Running at top speed was exhilarating. But it was also cathartic. Sozwik had so much pent-up emotion; frustration, confusion, loneliness, anxiety, helplessness, worry…etc. He knew that if he let it marinate in inaction, it would eventually manifest into paralyzing indecisiveness or even an ailment.

Sozwik slowed to a trot. As he began to descend the other side of the mountain, he heard it, a subtle *whoosh* in the distance.

"What's that?" He thought to himself, stopping and focusing his awareness as the next faint *whoosh* sound whispered in his ear. It seemed to be more machine-like than biological. The frequency that reached his ears reminded him of stories he heard about the wheeled vehicles The Guard used to transport zapixion in the earliest days of the Jyoti enslavement.

Sozwik's interest was so piqued that precaution was thrown out the window.

He followed the *whoosh*. It slowly got louder and louder as Sozwik made his way downhill and eventually onto level land. The sun was dipping under the hills, giving off its last rays of light, as he weaved through the trees.

Then he saw them… Lights.

The dual, luminous torches moved fast and were quickly out of sight. The *whoosh* sound transformed into a mechanical growl as the lights passed, then slowly back into a *whoosh* again. Another raced by a few seconds later.

Sozwik crept up to the opening of the forest, to the clear space where the lights were traveling.

It was a large clearing, like an open-top tunnel through the trees. And the ground was paved with a solid black coating, similar to what The Guard supposedly did on the routes which their wheeled vehicles traveled.

He heard another faint *whoosh*, which quickly morphed into a fast-approaching roar. Then Sozwik saw the lights, very clearly this time, and now there was no mistaking what it was.

"It's a vehicle!" Sozwik's mind screamed to him, in a mix of excitement and terror.

In a state of awe, Sozwik unconsciously stood up from his hiding place as the lights focused on him.

The car was now hurtling straight at him. It was a dark, shining exoskeleton of metal. The lights in the front looked like a pair of devious eyes intent on cutting him down.

Sozwik was a Jyoti caught in the headlights, completely frozen.

Right before hitting him, the vehicle jerked and swerved to the side.

The fast-flowing stream of time turned into a slow trickle. While movement seemed to take on a dreamy lethargy, Sozwik's mind was operating in rapid-fire mode.

As the vehicle took on its slow-motion swerve, Sozwik saw a human inside. He knew it was a female human by the long hair and delicate, yin features.

The human stared straight at him. They locked eyes for what was certainly an eternity. The river of time froze.

…

Her petite jaw was agape, stupefied with surprise. Her green eyes were wide open with fright. Sozwik felt his facial features behave similarly.

…

But behind all the shock, there was that sense of connectedness again. It was an even deeper underlying unity that he had felt with the human man.

…

Then the floodgates opened. Time surged forward. The car screeched and sped off and Sozwik found himself in the middle of the clearing, standing in a daze upon the solid black surface.

Instinct kicked in, and with a vigorous shake of his entire body, Sozwik released shock of the encounter and hurriedly hurdled his way back into the forest.

He traveled so fast that he outpaced his own thoughts. But they boomeranged back eventually.

"Only a few days on this planet and I've had two close encounters with humans. I don't think that I'm going out of my way to see them. And surely The Guard can't be tracking my every move through this stupid Top Rank Badge. Well, hopefully not… That woman though. The presence I felt was uncanny. Her energy was so familiar, almost too familiar, but I can't quite place it."

Sozwik wandered through the wilderness like movement itself would illuminate solutions to the unanswered questions of his inscrutable predicament.

Ω

At the magical hour of dawn, as the tide of light washed upon the shores of darkness, Sozwik stopped in his tracks on the crest of a rather large mountain. Something caught his attention.

Just below the horizon lay a great gray mass pulsating with smoke, noise, lights and chaotic electromagnetism. Everything about it repelled Sozwik, yet he was completely enthralled. He had never seen anything like it.

"A human village." The thought slipped in and bounced around in his mind.

Sozwik had an intuitive knowing that humans resided there, but the word village felt like a stretch, as its appearance and energetic signature were completely unlike that of Jyoti villages.

Tuning in his perceptions to the gray mass of condensed activity, individual aspects began to reveal themselves. First was the noise, which rumbled with a mass trumpeting of horns. Then the noise itself partitioned and he heard the chatter of countless humans. The voices were carried by an emotional wave of worry, fear, resentment and anxiety, which surged into Sozwik's psyche like a tide of psychic venom. Shirking the jarring disharmony for a moment, he zoomed in his auditory faculties even further. One individual voice broke through the rest. "I can't do this anymore." It was filled with feelings of disempowerment and regret. Feeling this human's despair like it was his own, Sozwik snapped back to his immediate surroundings.

Regathering himself, Sozwik shifted his focus to his vision. He fixed his inquisitive eyes upon on the gray lump on the land and zoomed in. In a green-then-gray blur of optical microscoping, clarity emerged in the image of a man sitting in front of a screen, palming his face with apparent agony. Then his vision zoomed out again and he pondered…

"Humans must be more horribly enslaved than the Jyoti. Yet I see no fences around their village…"

In deep, wordless thought, Sozwik continued to gaze at this strange human village from afar.

Then, for some reason, as he looked upon it for some time, his thoughts drifted towards his early training days with Goa…

Chapter 7
A Vision of Control

The Guard is referred to as such,

because the physical guards behave like bees in a hive, motivated by some unseen force. All the individual beings (although it's a stretch to call them "individuals") seem to be driven by the same pervasive force. This totality, or collective hive mentality, is known as The Guard.

The physical guards are strange creatures, stained with sameness and as mechanical as they are flesh and blood. The Guard ever-seeks control and hierarchy, fueled by an insatiable parasitic appetite.

Rumor has it that the force known as The Guard has laid waste to many planets, perpetuating the following cycle... It seeks to completely control each target planet and rule with technological might. But The Guard's lack of connection to everything else in existence eventually destroys the planet along with all life on it. Then it moves to the next, repeating this insatiable pattern of exploitation and seeking total control.

The Guard's basis of existence is ignorance, its goal is utter control, and its motivation is fear. In the Grand Unfoldment, The Guard is essentially the counterforce to the universal nature of all things. It is a game of sorts, the ultimate test, to place the maximum number of limitations upon beings, and see what they're really made of when the going gets tough. The Guard's wrath actually catalyzes the process of Universal Evolution, though only those beings who see the Big Picture can perceive this.

The servants of The Guard, also known as "the guards," are the manifestations of The Guard in physical form (as The Guard manifests itself on all dimensions below it). At this time, the guards were of two humanoid species (humanoid being a loose classification of bipedal creatures that use tools and have some form of language). The first were the Trakul, extremely keen and cunning beings, preferring to manipulate from the shadows. The second host species were the Harka, orcish brutes who acted as the strong-arm of The Guard.

Both types of guards lacked any sense of empathy towards other beings. Their only connection is The Guard itself, which consciously separated from the rest of existence many ages ago. Because of this disconnect, The Guard continues its pattern of laying planets to waste. Instead of working with the planet and its species, The Guard seeks complete control. And complete control is the opposite of life (as Universal Evolution is based upon the principles of growth and freedom), so it inevitably leads to planets becoming dead and desolate, unable to support any life (including The Guard, ironically).

Remember that planets are living beings as well. When a planet is laid to waste, it's akin to the death of any creature. A barren planet is like a dead body, though it takes much, much longer to "decompose" and join again with everythingness.

And speaking of planets…

Ω

At this point (during Sozwik's lifetime), Earth was the only other planet (in addition to the Jyoti's home planet of Seren) still under the control of The Guard. It had become the "planet of freedom" for the Jyoti because it was similar enough to Seren and had prevalent areas of undisturbed wilderness.

Beings were deliberately kept oblivious to these facts through many means. The Guard's modus operandi is secrecy and deception.

Due to a complicated knot of factors, The Guard did not simply kill Jyoti or take steps to eliminate the species as a whole. In some twisted, ironic way The Guard actually depended on the Jyoti. The Guard was also peripherally aware that the Jyoti were somehow in perpetual communication with each other, though it didn't know exactly how. This was the cause of both great interest and great fear within the hierarchy.

Enslavement of the Jyoti was a semi-recent phenomenon. The Jyoti had always lived in freedom and harmony until about four generations before Sozwik's birth. Even the idea of weapons seemed but a phantasmagoric whisper to the Jyoti.

The Guard located the precious mineral zapixion on Seren, which it so desperately needed. Zapixion was used to produce something akin to nuclear power as energy sources for its ships. The Guard is backwards in this sense too, because at this point in the Grand Unfoldment, all other galactic travelers were using UVE (Universal Vacuum Energy), which was infinitely abundant, clean and, once set up, never required any additional input.

In earlier years, The Guard invaded planets for gold (like they did with Earth), hoarding it and using it to fix the atmospheres of the planets it raped, to keep them habitable for its minions and slave populations. But The Guard had destroyed so many planets that its servants were now mostly relegated to a fleet of enormous starships, roaming like rogue pirates of the Universe.

By some puzzling fork in the road of fate, Seren held the gift and the curse of The Guard's highly coveted zapixion. The inevitability came to fruition, of course, and The Guard invaded.

This was a mission of desperation for The Guard, as it was backed into a corner - and we all know that predators are most dangerous when backed into a corner. The Guard was also apprehensive of the Jyoti, adding to its treacherous distress. Because the word around the cosmos was that, though they were peaceful beings, the Jyoti were the most robust and agile humanoids in the known Universe. The takeover could be disastrous, but it was a risk The Guard had to take.

Because its fate rested upon Seren's zapixion reserve, The Guard only wished to hold the Jyoti down long enough to extract its prize. It wanted to obtain a nice stockpile of zapixion and get out with minimal damage. "A nice stockpile" is relative, of course. The Guard, often drunk with greed, has been known to overstretch itself and insolently extend its unwelcomed stays.

The Jyoti, true to their benevolent nature, initially welcomed The Guard upon its arrival and offered food and wood carvings to the guards, like they would any other visitors. And the guards gobbled the food and smashed the wood carvings, like they would to any other host.

The Guard was only out for zapixion, by any means necessary. It was also not equipped to mine it (surprise, surprise). Though the minions it sent were rather large brutes, they couldn't survive in what we would call a "healthy" atmosphere for long. The guards had evolved over millions of Earth years in the most toxic environments imaginable, chemical wastelands cloaked in blankets of smoke and all-pervasive radiation.

The Guard blocked off the valley with a giant red forcefield fence and forced the Jyoti to mine zapixion from the womb of the mountains.

The Jyoti knew that a violent rebellion would be futile against The Guard, as it would likely lead to the extinguishment of their entire race. They also intuited that the collapse of The Guard was both imminent and inevitable when enslaving a race like theirs. The Jyoti had abilities that were unfathomable (and unperceivable) to The Guard, so its control was that of a clumsy polar bear chasing an arctic hare on thin ice.

In the early days of the enslavement, many of the more rebellious Jyoti organized noncompliance movements, but these were swiftly crushed. The Guard would simply annihilate all protestors on the spot, in cold blood.

So, the Jyoti took to a more long-term game. They continued their lighthearted, festive ways, despite the hardship, knowing that their rising sun was slowly illuminating the darkness.

The backbone of the Jyoti culture was the tradition Wakanry. The Wakans, as the practitioners of Wakanry were called, were the vessels through which the Jyoti's esoteric traditions were passed down. The closest thing to a Wakan on Earth is what humans call shamans; each essentially being the spiritwalkers and medicine-folk of their respective cultures. Sadly, the Wakan wisdom was gradually disappearing with each successive generation of enslaved Jyoti.

By using Earth as the planet of freedom, The Guard could still keep a watchful eye on the freed Jyoti. It provided an opportunity to study how they behave on their own accord.

But more importantly, the infinitesimally small number of freed Jyoti gave the masses — confined to a small valley in the heart of Seren — the hopeless hope of believed freedom that can keep a species indefinitely enslaved.

There were also rumors that The Guard was using freed Jyoti for some of their hardly known but infamous geneticreature experiments on Earth.

Earth had been an experimental testing ground of The Guard's for some time. Humans, who are similar to the Jyoti, but diminutive in comparison, and with far less hair, were The Guard's "prized creation" as they called it. However, The Guard only tweaked the DNA of a previously created version of humans.

This genetically hijacking was a domestication of sorts, which is why humans as we know have mostly been kept contained within city areas. Because of this, vast tracts of wilderness lay untouched. This set-up on planet Earth provided an opportunity for secret projects in underground bases and remote locations. It also created a sort of free-range, zoological park system, starring the "free" Jyoti. On top of this, The Guard arrogantly thought it had created an effortless separation between city-bound humans and the Jyoti of the deep wilderness. As long as both acted predictably, according to their respective programming, control could go on indefinitely.

Ω

Just as The Great Star ever gives off light, The Guard ever deceives. And the dark light of The Guard scorches those it oppresses into the charring inferno of control.

The Guard had managed to keep the Jyoti enslaved for four generations with a combination of physical barriers (the forcefield field) and intense programming.

The Guard only resorted to physical barriers out of desperation. Because blatant slavery can only last so long before rebellion inevitably occurs. But covert slavery (when the enslaved do not realize it, as they did with humans), can go on indefinitely.

The Guard's mission on Seren was a scramble for zapixion. With this, The Guard applied their short-term plan of control which consists of physical barriers and "youth curriculum."

The Jyoti had only heard about the concept of slavery through folklore, and most thought of such an obscene disgrace to freedom as fictional, a mythological nightmare. This is why the majority of Jyoti were paralyzed with shock and disbelief when The Guard appeared on Seren with the intent of enslavement.

The Guard's "youth curriculum" consisted of repeatedly showing the youth "training videos" on screens. This programming was specifically designed to subtly condition each Jyoti to concede their will to authority figures (The Guard), take orders without question and accept the mandatory mining of zapixion everyday as "that's just the way life is." It was an insidious programming based upon fear and subservience. This was easy for The Guard to implement, as they used the same videos for every other race they enslaved for mining. All they had to do was make it compulsory and play it for the youth each morning on a holographic screen projected in the center of the village.

Of course, there was fierce resistance to this at first, and many Jyoti hid their youngn's in attempt to avoid the programming. But after several public killings, they had no choice but to acquiesce.

The youth curriculum was mandatory for the Jyoti from birth through age six. The Guard wished to mold their impressionable minds. By age seven, all Jyoti were sent to work in the mines.

The programming consisted of images and words spoken in the hideous tongue of The Guard. It was all cunningly designed to penetrate the subconscious mind and implant beliefs of subservience, obedience, fear, self-doubt and anything else to create a population that was more easily controlled.

Though most of their thought-speak (what humans would call telepathic communication) remained intact — as this was beyond the reach of The Guard's programming — it made them far more obedient, docile and domesticated than their once-free ancestors. By Sozwik's generation, as the programming suggested, most Jyoti viewed enslavement as "just the way life is." Isn't that the most mentally ensnaring perilous plight of a species?

The Guard's physical presence become less frequent in each subsequent generation, save for when an overly rambunctious Jyoti was caught roaming outside of the valley and put to death (which had also become rarer, thanks to the programming).

There was another important factor though. The Guard was intrigued by the Jyoti, and jealous of them in many ways. From their dynamic athleticism to how they seemed to communicate without the use of words. The Jyoti might be of use to The Guard, though it didn't exactly know how. This is why some were granted "freedom" to go to Earth. It was a ploy to study "free-roaming" Jyoti in their natural ways.

Earth was the perfect choice for this "freedom," as it was under control of The Guard, and so similar to their natural habitat on Seren.

But The Guard didn't take any risks and made sure any Jyoti that went to Earth had to be thoroughly programmed so as not to cause any trouble. The Guard had haughty confidence in its programming, as it had worked so well with humans.

The orphan child of The Guard's control and conniving curiosity was the Top Rank. Only those Jyoti who caught The Guard's interest were recruited for Top Rank. The intriguing specimens, if you will. But there couldn't be any breaking the mold, which is why the Top Rank were also the most thoroughly indoctrinated.

By the fourth generation, the Top Rank was looked at with veneration. And freedom was but a fleeting glimmer of hope for a suppressed population.

The Top Rank program was a more thorough version of the youth curriculum. Achievement of the position of Top Rank was simply determined by accumulating over 1,000 "Instruction Sessions" as The Guard called it, as well as having no complaints regarding your work in the zapixion mines.

The program consisted of the most extensive programming shown on hypnotizing screens for hours on end. Sozwik was a hidden anomaly within the Top Rank, who Goa referred to as "The Inside Jyoti" during their Wakan training. Through Goa's mentorship, Sozwik was able to fly under the radar of The Guard throughout the ascension (more like descension) to Top Rank.

As per the nature of the system, Sozwik's Top Rank mates were not like him in the slightest, as they were thoroughly indoctrinated. He could see his classmates getting more brainwashed by the day as he proceeded through the Top Rank program.

Ω

Sozwik obviously received the programming as well, but was also secretly trained in Wakanry by Goa. This counterbalancing force was what kept Sozwik's head above water. The water, in this case, being the tempestial ocean of Top Rank programming.

Over the years, Goa had developed strategies to minimize the effects of programming, and even how to reverse most of its effects afterward. The reversal strategies were new territory in Wakanry, as the free elders never had to deprogram in the first place. So essentially, Sozwik received a crash course in Wakanry blended with Goa's experimental counter-programming techniques.

At this point, Goa was the foremost torchbearer of the Wakan tradition among the Jyoti, as he was exposed to both the free ancestors and a lifetime of enslavement. Goa was the living bridge between freedom and slavery.

Sadly, the enslavement was turning Wakanry into a dying craft. Others were learned in the Wakan tradition (like Sozwik's parents and a few others), but none, save Goa, were true masters who could effectively teach the highest levels of the craft.

Though Sozwik's training was fruitful, it was excruciatingly intense at times, as his limits were continuously stretched.

One of these strange defining moments will never be forgotten. From day one, Goa knew Sozwik had great potential and was quite hard on him as a result. Sozwik was young at the time. Goa was teaching him "stillness among pressure" and had Sozwik attempt to meditate while he was doing his best to distract him. Sozwik, who tended to put a lot of pressure on himself, broke down under this intense pressure and ran off.

Sozwik hid within the sanctuary of the deep woods and sat there crying. In that moment of pitiful self-doubt, he felt as if a spirit had stroked his cheek. He swatted at it, believing it to be a leaf or even Goa, but nothing was there. Annoyance gave way to awe as this non-physical something stroked his cheek again. It was a subtle touch, yet profound beyond comprehension and filled with all-embracing compassion. This gave him the spark of hope he needed to carry on. Sozwik picked his head up, gazed at the sky and felt the most overwhelming feeling of love. Actually, he felt as if he had literally become love itself.

This was the point of Wakan training; to bring you to a breaking point, and through intense pressure, transform coal into a diamond. Goa knew exactly what he was doing and let Sozwik have that time in the deep woods to himself. The next day, Sozwik came back to Goa a new version of himself, ready for the next level of training.

One of Goa's favorite sayings was, "A stronger version of yourself awaits you on the other side of your self-imposed barriers." And let me tell you, Sozwik's barriers were shattered countless times during his Wakan training under Goa. By the time Sozwik was 16 years old, dancing along the line of life and death was commonplace. As is the path of the Wakan master.

Though he was greatly wisened by his training, and probably the most physically capable Jyoti of his generation, Sozwik still had a sensitive side to him. At its worst, Sozwik would be extremely reactionary to any criticism and withdraw into himself. At its best, he was a being of such compassion and far more in tune with the phenomena of feelings than any male Jyoti Goa had ever met. This tendency towards sensitivity was simply part of Sozwik's persona in this lifetime, due in part to the peculiar alignment of stars at the moment of his birth.

The Jyoti had their own version of astrology, called Kitali, which they used as an "archetypal template" for individuals. It was not viewed as a fixed destiny, but more as a general insight into the predisposed strengths and weaknesses of individuals. Strengths of course, were leveraged, and weaknesses could be overcome through the study of Kitali.

Ω

Goa also trained Sozwik in using the vision-space. And through navigating these realms with Goa, Sozwik learned much about the nature of The Guard. But most importantly, he learned much about the nature of self.

Before Sozwik's first visit to the Jyoti vision space, Goa had given him a sagacious disclosure...

The Guard programs the brains of those it wishes to oppress because The Guard itself is a form of metaphysical virus. It is a distortion of the vision-space of a species, in which the distorted vision-space controls the species instead of the other way around. Its origins are rumored to be with the Trakuls, who are widely considered the most cunning species in the universe. Yet, their gift became their curse. The Trakuls became so absorbed in egoic mind-identification and neglected the compassion of the heart. This led to ubiquitous hierarchical systems, insatiable greed, the hoarding of resources and collectively perpetuated violence.

The mind is a problem-solver and therefore goes on finding problems. Problems are the very foundation of its existence, so species that are mind-dominant go on finding and/or creating problems. The mind also perceives all things as separate, finite and mechanical (as this is the best way to logically solve problems, of course). But everything is a balance, and those who let the mind use them, instead of using the mind, operate under a fear-based, scarcity paradigm.

The Trakuls greed reached a tipping point that, instead of individuals being greedy, the whole race eventually became physical manifestations of greed. The Guard then spread like a virus among several other species, including the Harka, which now make up the vast majority of The Guard's minions and are the nitwits we have to deal with on Seren.

It's also important to note that the Trakuls were master translators. All other species were kept divided through their different tongues. But the Trakul were hoarders of language and used it to their advantage. While most other species only spoke one language, the Trakuls spoke almost all. Combined with their malign cunning, the Trakuls' language prowess became another tool for their manipulation tactics. The Harka, the other arm of The Guard, were taught just enough of certain languages to do their job. So, it can be said that the Trakuls had become the brains of The Guard and the Harka were the brawn.

Ok, now back to the vision-space... These days, the fourth generation of slavery, very few Jyoti even have the ability to reach the vision-space. Our thought-speak is still intact with virtually everyone, but the programming somehow cut off most of our kin from the vision-space. However, there were times like after rituals and feasts, where most Jyoti would be in the vision-space during their sleep for the next few days after (it was quite entertaining to see some of them pop in for the first time, comically stricken with surprise). As you know, Sozwik, only a handful of us can deliberately enter the vision-space whenever we want.

This is providing a real problem for us Jyoti. Much crucial strategery, communication and sharing can take place in the vision-space. And since it's beyond the reach of time, one can do as much in the vision-space as one pleases and it all happens in the space between an inhale and exhale of the physical body. Wakan masters can shape an almost infinite number of things in the vision-space and inject all of it into one moment of physical reality. This is how powerful the vision-space is.

And this is The Guard's power as well, for it is a distortion of a species' vision-space. But even though it can't enter our vision-space yet (they're on a completely different frequency), its programming severs the connection between the species and its vision-space.

Even when a species is disconnected from its vision-space, the vision-space is still there. And this is where The Guard does its real work. The vision-space is inherently a realm of connection, being a collective space. But when a species is disconnected, they tend to fall victim to the fear-based paradigm of the mind. The vision-space is always being shaped by the species, so once a species hits a tipping point of the fear-based control paradigm, the vision-space mutates like a cancer and becomes The Guard. From here, the vision-space (now the mutation/virus called The Guard) controls the species and they become minions of The Guard, slaves to its malevolent will. It's incredibly difficult for any species to shake once their vision-space has gone rogue. No known species has accomplished this, though it's rumored that humans might have the capability.

The Guard can manifest on an individual level as well. This is when The Guard distorts one's mind and energy field to the degree where it starts to control them. Of course, this control is much easier when a species is under deep programming and limited in awareness.

Some of the Jyoti of old, being well-versed in vision-spaces, could even reach the resonance of other races. I have never done this, but some of the elders I learned from as a young'n claimed to have this ability.

The Jyoti vision-space manifests as a three-dimensional hologram, where we're able see the exact details of anything other Jyoti are explaining.

A few Jyoti on Earth have accessed the vision-space as well, though it's much more difficult from there. I'm still trying to pinpoint the exact reasons for that, though I have my speculations.

The tricky part is entering the vision-space at the same "time" as the Jyoti on Earth. It's difficult to organize as they have a different star system and time structure. So, I try to spend as much "time" as I can in the vision-space in order to glean information from the Jyoti on Earth, which happens to be my soul brother Paupo most of the time. He's the only Earth-bound Jyoti who accesses the vison-space consistently.

The Jyoti of the Wakan tradition are almost single-handedly holding the vision-space together, as each generation subjected to programming is driving the vision-space closer to the tipping point. It is rumored among some that the next generation would be the last straw that breaks the species. Yet I have faith that there are forces at work which will stop this momentum in its tracks.

Chapter 8
The Unseen War for the Jyoti Mind

Most difficult of all is what Sozwik endured to reach Top Rank.

The programming was overwhelming. Like the youth curriculum, the Top Rank curriculum was shown on the holographic screen in the center of the village on a daily basis.

The themes were similar to the youth curriculum, but it was more intense as the Jyoti watching it had already been exposed to the "warm-up" of the youth curriculum. And truthfully, if one were to watch one of the Top Rank programming videos without first going through the youth curriculum, they would be terrified and disheveled.

During his training with Goa, Sozwik had been able to "block out" the psychic intrusion of the youth curriculum by the time he was age five (Goa began training him at the age of four). Goa had also taught him to travel back into his memories and remove the implants within his subconsciousness. Sozwik was essentially a clean slate, a fully functioning Jyoti, though The Guard had no way of knowing this. This is why the onslaught of the Top Rank programming was excruciating for Sozwik.

Sozwik had to reach into the depths of his Wakan practices during each session. His Wakan Self (the self which is not programmed and in one's own power) was like a valiant warrior alone on a battlefield, bearing just a shield, and faced against hundreds of archers firing arrows non-stop for two hours straight (the length of the programming session). Sozwik's Wakan Self expertly blocked and evaded arrows day in and day out. Each session pushed Sozwik to the point of total exhaustion. Over the course of his 1,000 sessions, Sozwik had only been "pierced" 54 times by the arrows of programming. And he had to work with Goa to remove each of these implants one by one, for each was potentially deadly.

Ω

The process of removal was what humans would call "astral traveling" into parts of his own mind.

Sozwik would go into deep meditative states, facilitated by Goa, until his consciousness punctured the dimensional veil. From here, his mind was like a maze, with hundreds of doors. Behind some of these doors lurked the programming implants.

During the course of these sessions, Sozwik had to make sure each and every one of these doors were clear. Think of a special forces unit clearing the rooms of a building, making sure there are no enemies hiding out.

The programming implants that lay in hiding manifested themselves as the most hideous demons from the higher-dimensional perspective. Each time, the process of removal was an epic battle.

The stakes were high, for if Sozwik was defeated by any of these demons, his consciousness itself would become one, and the totality of his mind would be in full-fledged servitude of The Guard. Oh, it was a dangerous game. But it was the only way out.

One of these removals has now become a legend in the Wakan tradition…

Ω

It was Sozwik's 54th removal. He had thought the 53rd was his last, but the most deceptive and heinous avoid detection of all but the most experienced Wakan. This is why Goa facilitated these sessions, as he could often see what Sozwik couldn't, though he couldn't intervene inside Sozwik's own mind.

With Goa's encouragement, Sozwik broke through the interdimensional barrier and ventured through the labyrinth of his mind. Though he was in the ethers, Sozwik projected his usual form as a Jyoti; for he was highly adept with the Jyoti archetype and its athletic capabilities are virtually unmatched. (Everything takes one form or another in the ethers, but it's usually more according to one's state of consciousness than their actual physical form.)

After much exploration, Sozwik came across a door he had never seen before, deeply tucked away and shrouded in darkness. The fear that arose from just being near the door almost shook Sozwik out of his other-worldly state. But he centered himself.

Manifesting a crystal sword and shield into the grips of his hearty hands, Sozwik threw the door open. It was pure blackness and smelled of gut-wrenching decay. "Looks like nothing is in this horrid place," Sozwik thought.

But just before a sigh of relief arose, two humongous red eyes appeared out of the darkness in front of him.

The eyes penetrated him like poisonous daggers of fire. Sozwik was stunned as the gargantuan beast slowly moved towards him. The details of its shape were blanketed by darkness, but he could literally feel its monstrous size. The demon came excruciatingly close. Sozwik was still frozen, petrified as his gaze was locked in the trance of the huge red eyes.

A slimy limb, like a giant snake, curled around his right leg. "This is surely the end," seeped out of Sozwik's stunned consciousness.

Just as Sozwik had given up all hope, the voice of Goa thundered: "This is your house! Kick out that unwelcome visitor!"

The dark room rumbled…

Exploding out of his trance, Sozwik swung his sword down and severed the tentacle at his foot.

The demon was unfazed. It instantly grew the tentacle back and threw more limbs at him, like a tidal wave of repugnant flesh.

Sozwik sprung into a back-flip, blocking a tentacle with his shield as he was upside-down in the air, and landed like the hero he knew himself to be deep down.

In a burst of anger, the demon let out a terrifying, soul-shaking scream. The room shook. A rush of fear swept through Sozwik, but it didn't stick and passed over him this time.

Before the scream was even over, the monster leapt in the air. Sozwik looked up at the shadowy beast with flailing limbs coming down upon him. He frisbee-tossed his shield to the side, gripped his sword in both hands, and held it steadfastly above his head as he jumped upward to meet the beast. Instead of it crushing him, Sozwik sliced straight into the demon's underbelly, through its giant head and burst out the top like the explosion of a gruesome piñata.

Sozwik's feet hit the ground again and the room immediately transmuted into a space of golden-white light. There was no trace of the beast nor any of the heavy darkness it carried.

This was the moment Sozwik knew that his deprogramming work was completed.

He gradually eased himself back into his physical body and opened his eyes to see Goa eagerly smiling at him.

"It was fear itself," Sozwik muttered with immense relief. Not primal fear, or danger, that animals feel, but the programmed psychological fear that paralyzes the minds of intelligent beings.

"They say that the only thing to fear is fear itself," Goa exclaimed in a fit of relief. "But how many can say they slayed fear itself!?"

Sozwik let out the kind of tired smile that only comes from coming back from the brink of annihilation.

Goa continued, "You will still feel fear, doubt, anxiety and the like. But this will be your own. You have rid your mind of the unwelcome demon of fear programmed by The Guard. And I can say with certainty that your deprogramming is complete. Now it's time to do the real work of Wakanry."

Ω

After the utter hardships of deprogramming, Sozwik dove into the learning and practicing of many of the ancient Wakan ways.

Crucial to both Wakan training, and the existence of the Jyoti as a species, was their intimate relationship with plants.

The Jyoti of old had built a mutually beneficial relationship with the flora on Seren. In exchange for moving the seeds of the plants and not haphazardly cutting them down, the plants bestowed great knowledge upon the Jyoti. The mighty trees offered their expansive branches as homes, the quick-growing Kempo trees offered themselves as building material (which the Jyoti used for all their woodworking), and various other forms of vegetation offered themselves as food and medicine.

Like every core aspect of Wakanry, the relationship with plants had been slowly fading since the enslavement. Besides the few who were proficient in the Wakan ways, most Jyoti had a distant relationship with the plants, like an old friend who you still love but see terribly infrequently.

Goa explained the plants' reality to Sozwik like this: "Animals move in space. But plants move in time (or through the progression of events, as time is just a construct). Jyoti are plant-fueled animals who can move in both space and time. That is why we are the liaisons between worlds."

All Jyoti were in communication with at least some plants, even during Sozwik's lifetime. But it was usually limited to the trees they lived in and the plants of their garden.

Goa taught Sozwik how to communicate with any plant, create deep bonds with them and foster harmonious, synergistic relationships. Just through his initial training in Wakanry, Sozwik could already feel the unique energy of each plant wherever he walked. And if he focused on one, he would get subtle messages. Goa, however, gave him the tools to really dive deep.

A powerful skill that Goa taught Sozwik was how to receive 'downloads' of a tree's entire lifetime and its knowledgebase, simply by touching it.

"The first step is to bring yourself into a meditative state," Goa instructed one day in the most remote corner of the valley. "Use your breath to rise above the chaos of your thoughts. Only then can you hear wisdom of the plants." Sozwik did this without much difficulty, as it was a pillar of Wakanry that he practiced daily.

Goa continued… "Now walk slowly. Walk in a flowing feminine way, open to receive." Sozwik had a hard time doing this, as he had conditioned himself to always move fast and with purpose. Attempting to walk slowly caused a mental disconnect to arise and he was pulled back to the noisy realm of thought.

"Ugh," Sozwik grunted in frustration. "I can't walk like that."

"What do you mean? It's just walking. You're letting your habits control you. Shake out the mechanical patterning from your body and start over."

After a few more attempts, Sozwik was flowing through the forest with such grace that it felt like he was dancing with everything around him. The plants were speaking clearly to him, and he "understood" thousands of them simultaneously.

"That's where you want to be," Goa expressed with satisfaction. "Now, tune into the energy of a specific tree and see if it's calling back to you."

Sozwik felt a pull on his right side and his gaze met a tree that seemed so friendly.

"Place your hands upon its trunk and listen," Goa softly instructed.

Flowing to the tree like a stream to a lake, Sozwik greeted the sagacious being with a nod of gratitude and placed his hands upon its sturdy trunk. In an instant, Sozwik's consciousness was flooded with information. Innumerable waveforms of knowledge rippled through him, and epiphanies fell upon his head like drops of rain. When the download was completed, the tree simply said, "This world is a trip, huh? Well, pleasure to meet you, Sozzy."

Sozwik lowered his hands from the tree and stared up at it, mouth agape in complete disbelief.

"And that's just the tip of the iceberg…" Goa chuckled with a wink and a smile.

Chapter 9
Finding the Others

Later that day,

when he finally shook off the close call with the car, Sozwik let his intuition guide him to an open hilltop; a natural observatory with a 360-degree view of the surrounding land and sky above.

Sozwik stood with his vision fixated on a star shining straight above him. Even in the daylight he could see it. Was it Seren? He held a hopeless hope it was so. Same as the hopeless hope for freedom that most Jyoti so desperately clung to, knowing in their heart of hearts it would never come to be.

The thought of Seren reignited Sozwik's desire to reach out and connect with his brethren and sistren. Though he was as adept as any Jyoti, few had ever found themselves in such an isolated ordeal. This weighed on him. Sozwik felt lost, forlorn, and floundering without the omnipresent connection he was so accustomed to on Seren. Because he knew nothing else, he had taken that ubiquitous communion for granted, until now.

Now he truly understood the meaning of a piece of Wakan wisdom that always baffled him… "One is oblivious to the ocean they are swimming in until they are hooked by some unseen force and thrust into an alien environment. Only then can one see their original world as it is."

An urge simmered within Sozwik's body. It became greater and greater until it was an insatiable desire, a desperate longing that wholly possessed him.

Sozwik had to communicate with the other Jyoti on Earth. He felt their presence since first arriving, but in such a subtle way that he only realized it in hindsight.

According to what he heard through Goa, there were around 20 Jyoti on Earth, as four generations had been granted freedom. The Jyoti lived incredibly long lives, about 1,000 Earth years on average. This seems impossible from the human perspective, but time is relative (and optional in some cases) and the Jyoti body is far more durable than the human body.

It is estimated that the first Jyoti were sent to Earth approximately 2,000 Earth years prior to Sozwik (remember, Seren is on a completely different timetable than Earth as well). So only a few Jyoti passed away during this time period; unless they were killed, which is always a dark possibility with The Guard involved.

Sozwik knew he had to enter the Jyoti's vision-space if he was to communicate with any Jyoti, on Earth or Seren. With his Wakan training, this energetic syncing came naturally to him on Seren, but from Earth it was as difficult as catching a nycono at night. He was at a loss.

Searching through the rolodex of his mind for a possible solution, Sozwik teetered on the tightrope between fear and faith. He breathed, steadied himself, and as he kept moving, hints of possible solutions began to arise. It was like picking up on the faint clues at the start of a scavenger hunt, knowing (somehow) that it will lead where you need.

Sozwik remembered what Goa had once said. There was no sure-fire way to access the vision-space from Earth. And every Earth-bound Jyoti who had accessed it had done it differently. But the core of each strategy was somehow getting in touch with the energetic signature of Seren and using some form of Wakan meditation.

"But what exactly can I do?" Sozwik pondered. He allowed himself to relax for a moment in an attempt to inveigle an idea into his mind. It worked. An idea almost instantaneously percolated through. "The plants themselves will bring me a solution."

With each step he took, Earth's sun crept higher and higher in the sky. High noon, in all of its shadowless glory, was upon him. His walk became more of an autumn daydream than a mere stroll through the woods.

Sozwik breathed deeply until he was centered and graciously walked a winding path through the forest, knowing one of the plants would greet him with the answer.

And sure enough, one of them did. At eye level, on one of the larger trees, was a viscous stream of sap.

"That's it! Krit! I'll make Krit," Sozwik excitedly exclaimed to himself.

This was all well and good, but he did not know how to find medicine plants for the concoction, for surely none of Seren's medicine plants existed on Earth. Disappointment dragged Sozwik's excitement back into the ocean of emotion. But the tide giveth as much as the tide taketh away, for Sozwik's hopeful enthusiasm washed upon the shores of his mind but a moment later.

"There must be sister-plants though. Seren and Earth are remarkably similar."

Not knowing how else to find them, Sozwik figured he might as well ask the tree. There is actually a funny old Wakan saying, "You might as well ask a tree." This waggish phrase surely came to Sozwik at this point. How could it not?

"Hey friend," Sozwik said to the tree. "Can I consult with you?"

Sozwik stilled himself and feeling a "yes" emanating from the tree, he placed his hand on its trunk and instantly received a message:

"The plants speak to those who listen. Thank you for being respectful. We have great reverence for the compassionate ways of your species. Everything you need for your recipe is here. Walk with heightened awareness and the right plant will indeed summon you."

"Thank you," replied Sozwik, letting his hand slide down and gently stroke the tree in a heartfelt goodbye.

Sozwik began to walk and listened intently as he scanned the adorable flora around him. After a few minutes, he felt a presence that became stronger and stronger with each step.

There it was, straight ahead. It was a humungous tree that, despite its compelling size, had a feminine, inviting charm. Decorated in curving, green vines, the tree appeared as a goddess of the forest.

There was no doubt in Sozwik's mind that this was the tree he would use. Walking up to it, Sozwik placed his hand on its smooth brown trunk, as if they were long lost lovers. The tree's reciprocation was felt by Sozwik through a wave of loving energy washing over him.

With a smile, he began to climb her. Sozwik reached his right arm up, extended and strong, and clasped onto a sturdy branch. Tensing his whole body, he hoisted himself up in an explosion of power. When his rib cage was flush with the branch, he threw his elbow overhead with lightning quick speed and pushed upward. The momentum allowed his free hand to catch an even higher branch, where the awesome motion was done again. Sozwik repeated this back-and-forth, one-handed muscle up with such powerful grace that it looked like he wasn't fighting gravity, but pulling the Earth down. In a matter of moments, Sozwik broke through the canopy and could see the other treetops below him. He had picked a truly admirable tree to climb.

On one large branch, a batch of leaves looked particularly friendly. The leaves were large, about the size of Sozwik's hand; and a deep, healthy green. They took on an oval-like shape that came to a modest point at both ends. The leaves were textured with subtle, wave-like ribs which gave them a pleasant disposition.

Sozwik felt a message come from the tree: "Here you go." He projected a "thank you," showing deep appreciation for the tree's generous offer to him.

Sozwik reached out and gently plucked the batch of leaves. Then, after a sacred pause, he nodded in gratitude before climbing back down.

Ω

A small cave near the great tree came to be Sozwik's impromptu laboratory.

Sozwik fashioned a makeshift fermentation device, using two carved chambers of wood. He put the tree sap inside and left the device near a small fire, which he kept constantly smoldering. Because of the clever construction, the fermented tree sap would slowly drip into a concave rock that acted as a bowl.

The fermentation process would take several rises and sets of Earth's mighty Sun. So Sozwik passed the time by climbing more mountains, testing his physical prowess, and sharpening his meditation abilities (to better prepare for his impending launch into the vision-space).

He also went to work on carving a beautiful wooden chalice, complete with the symbolism of old. Sozwik shaped it with elegant curves. It vibrantly displayed the symbols of the elements as well as the Jyoti symbol for Seren. Krit was always drunk out of wooden chalices. It was considered an essential part of the ritual. A handmade chalice, crafted with love and graced with powerful symbolism was said to enhance the positive effects of Krit.

When the tree sap was ready, Sozwik mixed the ingredients inside the sacred vessel. First were the medicinal plants he had collected. With a rock, he ground them on the bottom of the chalice. Next was the tree sap, which he scooped on top of the plant matter. Then he brewed a tea, infused with herbs he had picked nearby, within the heated rock he had used for the dripping tree sap. When the tea was sufficiently warm, Sozwik gently poured it into the chalice. The twisting stream, connecting the vessels to and from which it was poured, glowed in the cave light. After a bit of stirring with his finger and a smirk of gratitude (a Jyoti blessing technique), the Krit was complete.

Sacred chalice in hand, which he held like a proud father would hold an infant, Sozwik made his way back to the sacred hilltop which had previously caught his attention. The natural observatory held such a welcoming, cheerful energy. Because of this, it would be the perfect place to partake in the Jyoti ritual. With a true sense of knowing, Sozwik said to himself, "This will be my connection point to the others."

Sozwik slowly sipped the Krit as he soaked in the splendid scenery. The process of drinking Krit was a meditation in and of itself. With a subtle spiral movement of his hand, Sozwik made the Krit swirl and emit its herbal, aromatic fragrance. He breathed it in through his nose, cherishing the smell. Placing the chalice on his rugged lips, he took a small sip, letting the Krit pool in his mouth. The soft liquid texture was pleasing. The taste was delicately sweet with a hint of bitterness. With a relaxed flip of the tongue, he graciously swallowed, allowing the sacred liquid to slide down his throat. As the Krit's warming sensation radiated through his body, Sozwik drew in a deep breath, closing his eyes.

He did this, with each sip, until the Krit was finished. Then Sozwik opened his eyes, and the colors were already more vibrant, sounds were crisper, and reality was realer than real.

Settling himself into comfortable seated position, Sozwik began chanting. He repeated the chant, "I am all, all is I," in an ancient Wakan tongue, long forgotten by most Jyoti.

Sozwik's conscious awareness slowly expanded beyond the physical realm, like the inflation of an interdimensional balloon. His physical body faded gradually into invisibility. When fully in the vision-space, the physical body, though still "there," begins to vibrate beyond the spectrum of visible light. A curious phenomenon.

Sozwik felt himself poking through the otherworldly layers of existence. As the realization engulfed him, Sozwik felt an ethereal doorway open. He stepped through. The living antenna known as Sozwik was now tuned into the vision-space, the Jyoti station of the celestial radio.

Chapter 10
The Inside Scoop

Sozwik instantly felt the presence, that distinct wise yet whimsical vibe of gathered Jyoti.

The "doorway" he had stepped through led to what felt like the Jyoti room in the divine mansion of the Otherworld. He was in the Jyoti vision-space.

It was like joining a conference call. Yet the exchanges were more subtle than physical voices. It was more like a group thought exchange.

Serendipitously, Paupo, who was also on Earth, happened to be there. This was peculiar. He had never encountered them in the vision-space before. Goa, on the other hand, was not there, as Sozwik would have expected.

The council members Olea and Fala were also there. They were the only Jyoti on Seren in the vision-space.

Sozwik projected a greeting and was met with a pleasant welcoming. The other Jyoti broke into a traditional hymn, celebrating the arrival of their brother.

They asked about his experience on Earth so far, with genuine interest. Sozwik took the ethereal floor and told his short tale of Earthly experience so far; exploring the wilderness, the hunter, the berries, the woman in the car, how he was able to connect into the vision-space…etc.

"Krit was a good choice, Young Sozwik," said Paupo, the eldest of the Jyoti on Earth, who was often referred to as "Uncle." He was every Jyoti's wise uncle, astoundingly dependable, always lending a helping hand and ever available for counsel.

Paupo was Goa's main source of information on Earth because he was the only one who accessed the vision-space regularly. Sozwik had received much of Paupo's information second-hand through Goa, but now he was at the source.

Uncle Paupo continued. "Krit was an effective means of grounding into the Jyoti channel and accessing our vision-space."

He then went on to explain to him what was happening on planet Earth.

Sozwik learned that the Jyoti of Earth were dispersed throughout the wilderness of the planet, tucked in the untouched nooks of Mother Earth. Far more robust than humans, the Jyoti were well-suited for the most remote and extreme places of Earth. Paupo secretly connected with several of them on a regular basis. Sometimes even in the flesh, which was as dangerous as chasing a nycono off a cliff. The Guard strictly forbade physical contact. And The Guard was ever watching.

All of the Jyoti thoroughly enjoyed free roaming around Earth. After being contained within the valley on Seren their whole lives, it felt exhilarating to not be confined within geographical boundaries. Deep down, the Jyoti didn't like any boundaries, be them physical, mental or spiritual.

Although the Jyoti enjoyed their "freedom" in many ways, it was a bit isolating for such a social species. Sozwik already experienced this firsthand. The Jyoti of Earth all yearned for connection, whether it was with each other or any other being. And for this reason, they cherished whenever another was in the vision-space.

The longing for connection was also why covertly watching humans had become the unspoken pastime of the free Jyoti. They would openly discuss their observations of humans in this informal, vision-space forum.

After the introductions and a host of informal side conversations, they got down to business. Uncle Paupo took the ethereal floor to elaborate to Sozwik…

Ω

We knew you were searching, Sozwik, so we arranged as many hints as we could from this vision-space, hoping to reach you.

We've reached out through the vision-space after each generation came to Earth, and you're the only one who has answered the subtle call so far. Goa has taught you well, Sozwik. But sadly, he is not here now, as he has physical matters on Seren to attend to.

I'm sure he's told you much, but I will tell you my story nonetheless, for full disclosure is of utmost importance at this time.

I was sent to planet Earth four generations ago, among the first group of Jyoti to be granted freedom.

When I arrived, there was even more untouched wilderness on this planet.

Humans have developed their sprawling civilizations at a rapid pace, for better or worse.

Much of it is due to the pervasive influence of The Guard and we are beginning to see the repercussions of it. Even in the remote areas we inhabit, our communication channels are being blocked.

The electromagnetic pollution of planet Earth is an unseen hand, clouding our telepathic clarity in some regions. This frequency pollution is in the form of radiation and electromagnetic smog. One big culprit that we've identified is what the humans refer to as "cell phone towers." Those things are like firewalls projected out for many miles in every direction. Apparently, humans have had their thought-speak suppressed for so long that they need a silly buzzing device to communicate with one another over any distance. Because this "noise" was spread throughout most of Earth, it's been even more difficult than before to tune into the vision-space. On top of this, it has also affected our own thought-speak. We have not heard from some of our folk here for several Earth years. This is disconcerting, to say the least.

Humans are but pawns of The Guard at this point. Yet this wasn't always so.

Shortly after my arrival, I encountered a human elder. The man was called a "shaman." One who possessed rare wisdom. These men are essentially the Wakans of humanity.

I was exploring a lake, nestled between two beautiful peaks. I must have been distracted by the scenery because as I came out of the woods near the lake, I heard, "Hello, elder brother." The human was sitting on a cliff, overlooking the lake. His eyes were closed, and his long, black hair was gently flowing in the calm breeze coming off of the lake.

He had not spoken to me, but used thought-speak. The man, still facing the lake, gestured in a friendly manner for me to join him. I hesitantly obliged, only because I could strongly feel his benevolence. I sat next to him in meditation, and he told me the story of man.

The shaman explained how humanity as it exists today is intimately tied to The Guard (though he referred to The Guard as "The Parasite," which is quite fitting indeed). As you know, The Guard is clever, but short-sighted. This is why it gets itself into sticky situations, and although it seems powerful sometimes, its demise is inevitable.

The Guard was operating almost exclusively through the Trakul race then, which the shaman called the "Naki." The Guard had destroyed the atmosphere of Ribo, the Trakul's home planet. While The Guard would typically just move on to the next planet, the instinctive stubbornness of the Trakul race won over and it was decided to keep Ribo as the home-base of The Guard. But the atmosphere had to be fixed in order to prevent runaway planetary warming and preserve the Trakul species (The Guard's precious host).

The solution was the ever-coveted mineral gold. They would create a blanket of gold particles around Ribo, which would act as an artificial atmosphere.

The nearest planet with a significant gold supply just so happened to be Earth. The Guard located this quickly of course, as pirating planetary resources is one of its specialties.

On a scouting mission, The Guard (through the vessel of the Trakuls), investigated the life forms on Earth. This was during what is called the Cretaceous Period on Earth, where dinosaurs were the dominant life-forms. Seeing how gigantic and dangerous these creatures were, The Guard knew the Trakuls couldn't survive with those monsters about, so it made quick work of the beasts by engineering a cataclysm and redirecting a meteor at Earth.

The Trakul species is well-known for redirecting rogue debris (meteors, asteroids and comets) to either avoid or create planetary destruction. They actually prevented one from destroying their own planet in the years before they were under the dominion of The Guard.

Since the Trakuls aren't very physically hearty, as they're more mind than body, they loathed mining gold themselves. Earth's atmosphere was also difficult for the Trakul, and they had to wear "Earth-suits" most of the time. The Trakuls had become almost entirely technological, their planet like a big slab of concrete with gray skies. So, they were adapted to what we would call a polluted environment.

Before long, the old Trakul stubbornness kicked in and those sent to the mines revolted against their higher ups. Not much was done and Ribo's atmosphere was almost completely obliterated at this point. So, it was decided that they had to find someone else to mine the gold.

A million Earth years is the equivalent of about 55 years on Ribo, as it's on the outer arm of an extremely fast spinning galaxy. This is also why The Guard has been playing such a long-term game through the Trakul. They live exponentially longer than other races. So, mammals evolved over the course of this time on Earth after the engineered cataclysm. The Guard paid little attention to them though, until the need for mining became urgent.

The Guard mixed the Trakul DNA with the most advanced apes (or so it thought) on Earth at this time, to create a more able-bodied, yet less intelligent (so it thought again), creature for the purpose of mining gold.

By the time the necessary amount of gold was harvested, The Guard was drunk with greed and saw newfound value in the humans. The most advanced Earth apes seemed to be connected to an even greater civilization of ages long ago. Humans have existed previously on Earth, though slightly different and in a highly advanced state (of that story even the shaman knows only vague speculations). Deciding not to wipe the humans out after the mining, The Guard brought the Trakuls back to Ribo and now had another race, humans, under its dominion.

The Guard is extremely cunning, and its nature is deception. Though it uses physical slavery in the short-term, it knows that any slave race will inevitably rise if the slavery is blatant and forced. The Guard's essence, its very being, is the subtle tactic of mental slavery. Once a species' vision-space has fully mutated into The Guard itself, it has total control and acts as a hive mentality which the hive (species) simply follows. How will a race free itself if it knows not of its slavery?

Because modern humans were basically birthed by The Guard, their vision-space was already distorted (and virtually inaccessible to most humans) and their civilizations developed according to The Guard's template.

The Guard provided humans with the foundations of civilization (language, culture, architecture, etc.) according to the structure of the Trakul civilization. In doing this, the framework of human society would develop under the paradigm of The Guard. Fear would be the underlying motivating force, being mind-dominant would beget a separation mentality and engineered scarcity would amplify the fear and separation, creating a conducive environment for control.

The vision-space of humans, though mutated into the "virus" of The Guard, contained a bubble of the arcane wisdom of the enigmatic golden age which existed even before The Guard. Some humans were able to tap into this and access the mysterious, ancient ways of what the shaman called Quondam Humans (or humans that existed in high states of consciousness in previous ages). At first this occurred by chance, but over time these ways of tapping into "the space within the vision-space" was refined. The Guard, in its blind arrogance, is still, to this day, unaware of this "bubble." So even though The Guard appears to have complete control, an underground esoteric community has existed since the dawn of humanity.

This is why humans can seem so stupid, gullible, and brutish most of the time, but then have moments of wisdom and understanding as great as any race in the physical dimension. They're the adopted children of The Guard whose previous life is an unseen power flying far below (or above?) the radar.

Human history is among the hardest to decipher as it's littered with the lies and deceptions of The Guard.

There are whispers that The Guard's genetic "creation" of humans is merely them taking credit for what more advanced beings did, which was the creation of Quandum humans for the purpose of reaching divinity. Again, both narratives are presented to show you how manipulated human history is.

The shaman also explained how The Guard was controlling Earth from the shadows. It gave humans their religions, which are distortions of inherent divine truth for purposes of control, because The Guard itself is the distortion of a vision-space.

The hidden esoteric communities of humanity, however, were able to access the divine through traditions similar to Wakan practices. Again, this probably has something to do with a collective subconscious memory from the unknown Quondam Humans.

The Guard also sought out to monopolize the raw materials on Earth. It uses different means of controlling planets depending on its host species. In this case, The Guard's main host species was the Trakul, who visit Earth every few hundred Earth years. The Trakuls placed humanity in "the squeeze," which is their code word for using scarcity to gain total control.

The two main aspects of "the squeeze" are energy and currency, what humans call "money."

It's necessary to create scarcity of energy and/or resources in order to control a population. If humans tapped into the abundant energy of "the vacuum" (or any of the other many "free energy" possibilities), they couldn't be controlled and might even shake The Guard off their back. The Guard, through the Trakuls, made sure that all human society operated based on finite resources (oil, coal, minerals…etc.). The various forms of pollution produced by this paradigm of resource usage also served the purpose of making Earth more habitable for the Trakuls. Some of the more ambitious Trakuls even wished to become overlords of the Earth.

Regarding currency, though currency is inherently neutral, the Trakuls devised a system (similar to their own) which syphoned wealth into the hands of a few. These few of course, were Trakuls themselves, hidden in the shadows of humanity's power structure.

There is so much going on between The Guard, the Trakuls and humans that your head would be spinning if I told you everything. I just want to give you enough information for you to understand the power structure we're dealing with on Earth, but not overwhelm you with every detail.

You see, my fellow Jyoti, most humans have become like the dogs, domesticated beasts completely dependent on their master (The Guard). The Jyoti, thankfully, are still like wild wolves. Yes, we've been in bondage for a few generations. But we haven't been fully domesticated yet and our vision-space is still functioning. There is hope still for us. And if there is hope for us, there is hope yet still for our human brothers and sisters.

The shaman man also pointed out that The Guard was directing humanity towards complete control. The Guard loves nothing more than control and domination. And it controls and dominates for the sake of control and domination itself. That's just what it does. The Guard is a vision-space parasite, sucking the life out of a species until there is nothing left, all the while jumping at any opportunity for a new host in the process. Its hunger is rapacious and insatiable.

He went on to elucidate about how the key to freedom lies in the true nature of everything, which is love, pure love. As you know, the natural state of a vision-space is love. But the distortion of a vision-space (aka The Guard) is fear, the antithesis of love. From the vision-space you have the trickle-down effect of that theme. This is why once The Guard takes over, you see the manifestations of fear everywhere in physical reality; scarcity, violence, war, division, hierarchy, control, deception…etc.

The Guard's only power is to trick others to give away their own power and succumb to its dominion. There are unexplored realms beyond the grasp of The Guard, as there are always a few of every species who, against all odds, buck against The Guard's agenda somehow.

I still have more questions than answers. What are these mysterious Quondam Humans of ages long forgotten? Is the bubble in the vision-space strong enough the stop The Guard? Can a race heal a vision-space through physical reality? Can we access, a higher space, something beyond the vision-space?

Those are questions yet to be answered. Neither I, nor the shaman man, nor Goa knows all there is to know. But we can continue to put the pieces together and gradually behold the Big Picture.

You see Sozwik, there is a lot at stake. We've been thrown in the middle of this saga and have the chance to play a pivotal role in its unfoldment.

Ω

When Paupo's long discourse came to an end, Sozwik was in a stupefied state of information overload, even though Paupo had spared some details. Despite the tidal wave of knowledge that hit him, Sozwik had a vague notion that, on some level, he was already beginning to make sense of it all.

The Guard's tactics, the Jyoti traditions and primal athleticism, the domestication of humans… It was all coming together in a faint feeling of understanding. Sozwik was still groping in the dark, yet he was beginning to form a picture of the nature of the beast.

In his heart, curiosity had won against fear and Sozwik's benevolent rebelliousness stood tall. He was now interested in how to pull the rug out from underneath The Guard (and if that was even possible at this point.). And he wanted to know how to stay under The Guard's radar, because he had a lingering feeling that he was being watched. At some of the places he visited on Earth, he felt the subtle presence of The Guard's watchful eye.

Sozwik explained this feeling to his fellow Jyoti. They addressed his curiosity with sly confidence. *How weren't they cowering in fear?*

The more experienced Jyoti had developed a strategy to avoid detection of The Guard. Many years of freedom on Earth drove these Jyoti to new levels of innovation. One major advantage they had garnered was the real intel on the tracking device sold to them as the "prestigious" Top Rank Badge.

Each Top Rank Badge emitted a unique signal which could be picked up by The Guard's master monitoring station. The Guard was studying every move of each free Jyoti in an attempt to discover their secrets as well as weak points to exploit.

On the plus side, there were a few regions on Earth where the signal would be disrupted. And certain Wakan meditation techniques changed or nullified the signal. But like entering the vision-space from Earth, a unanimous, sure-fire way was yet to be discovered.

The Jyoti had received much of this information from the boldest Jyoti to walk either Seren or Earth. This was a maverick named Utina. Utina had covertly developed friendships with many humans, some in high places of power.

She gleaned much information regarding The Guard. But her boldness had cost her her life. Utina was eventually caught and supposedly put to death by The Guard (though rumor has it they're keeping her imprisoned). Either way, the information she shared with the group was invaluable.

Along with the truth of the Top Rank Badge, much of the information that Utina revealed corroborated with the shaman man's knowledge. She also mentioned that most humans were unaware of The Guard (and even its host, the Trakuls) that controlled humanity from the shadows. The vast majority of humans were deliberately kept in comfortable ignorance as The Guard's master plan unfolded in front of their wool-covered eyes.

Utina also discovered that, even though there were many sightings of Jyoti, most humans did not believe they existed. The Jyoti were thought of as a fictional creature. But most native civilizations had intermittent encounters with the Jyoti and viewed them as a "cousin-species" to humans, as they were closer to nature and more similar in culture to the Jyoti.

Sozwik remembered hearing bits and pieces about Utina from Goa. She was an enigmatic legend. And it seemed as though most of her story hadn't even made it to the average Jyoti on Seren yet.

Paupo's knowledge was an expansive collection of Utina's revelations, his own experience and that of humans he had interacted with, like the shaman.

He had some more good news as well. "The Guard is becoming fearful every time they lose the signal from a Jyoti on Earth. Deep down, they know they can't control the Jyoti forever. Their entire reign is a string of desperate attempts to suppress the Jyoti through any means they can muster."

At this point, the vision-space was becoming glitchy. It seemed to be more unstable each day The Guard held the Jyoti in bondage. And there was still no definitive game plan, as even Paupo had more questions than answers.

"We don't yet know how to shake The Guard," Paupo said, wrapping up this vision-space meeting before it glitched out.

"But we do know how that pesky parasite operates. I wish I knew exactly what to do, but much knowledge is hidden, and our communication is heavily impaired. I request each of you to glean more knowledge about what we're facing, so we can soon come back and plot the inevitability of rebellion. Yes, there will have to be a rebellion. And what form it will take… Well, we will have to determine. Take care and exhibit caution. If The Guard knew how much we know, there would be great trouble. Use your intuition, call upon your heart, leverage the Wakan ways and tune into the vision-space as often as possible."

The seeds were now sewn. With an ethereal nod, the Jyoti broke communication and grounded back into their bodies.

Chapter 11
Reunited

The rain gently touched his face,

like an infinite amount of tiny angelic hands, bringing Sozwik out of his trance-like state and shading his body out of invisibility.

Sozwik found himself standing on the hill, with arms wide open. Sensory stimuli gently re-enveloped his consciousness and ushered him back to the realm of time and space.

Trying to assimilate the massive download he just received, Sozwik gazed at the dark gray clouds above. As their fluffy forms slowly moved over him, he thought about his situation, "What can I possibly do about all this?"

There was a response. Some sort of subtle magnetic pull. It felt more like a distant calling than anything. Sozwik couldn't yet put this vague sense of a mission to words, but he knew — on some level — that following this intuitive vocation would lead him where he needed to go.

Sozwik thought of what Goa said to him on the night before the freeing: "You don't need to see the whole path, just trust that the light of your consciousness will always allow you to see enough to continue moving forward. If you keep moving forward, you will eventually see the whole path."

As the sun's rays began to poke through the fading grayness above, Sozwik made his way down the hill.

Ω

Sozwik's thoughts flashed back to the human in the car. It was becoming clear now that, for some reason, he had to communicate with her.

Questions bubbled in his mind: "But how? How could I manage to communicate with her under The Guard's radar? And would she even be willing to communicate with me? What could she possibly know?"

He let this whirlwind of questioning pass over him, knowing it would all unfold perfectly if he were to simply surrender to faith and trust the calling.

Sozwik then began forming a plan in his head, using the "Past-Future-Space," or more commonly referred to as simply "Past-Future."

"Past-Future" is the Jyoti's system of memory and planning. It's similar to the vision-space in that it's a three-dimensional hologram, but it's fully based on one's personal imagination. Past-Future is created and experienced on the personal level, akin to the memory and imagination of humans. The sharpest of humans have photographic memory (and vague imagination), which are like two-dimensional snapshots. But other species like the Jyoti have holographic memory and imagination, which are three-dimensional, explorable models of intricate detail.

Sozwik spent some time viewing different scenarios as he would analyze a wooden carving. He turned them over and examined ideas from every angle with the keen eye of a master craftsman.

He went through dozens of situations, plans and methods, yet nothing seemed to feel right. Sozwik also felt a sense of urgency, for he knew he could waste no time in contacting this enigmatic human he had seen. If it were even a feasible option in the first place. But nothing he could think of was anywhere close to a reasonable plan.

"Perhaps thinking itself is the problem," Sozwik ironically thought to himself. A surge of frustration came over him and he gave up. All of Sozwik's plan spaces instantly cleared, but something peculiar happened…

He found his point of focus, not in a plan-space, but drifting above where he had been sitting, looking down at his body. As he gazed at his physical flesh vehicle, it slowly became cloaked in invisibility. Many species that often used vision-spaces and the like had evolved ways (such as invisibility) for their physical bodies to be hidden or protected while these phenomena occurred.

"Here we go again…" Sozwik hooted, as he had barely even reacquainted himself with physical world after the profound vision-space disclosure. He was journeying to other realms yet again. So is the life of a Wakan, they say.

Sozwik had been in vision-spaces often enough, but this was an entirely new experience. He had never seen the physical world from outside of his body before. His body was now veiled in intangibility, no longer seen at all. Realizing this, fear swept over him like a wave. Sozwik spun in a bodyless panic, confused and frightened. He needed something to hold onto, something to relieve this terror of non-existence. Not knowing why, he began repeating the mantra of personal truth: "I am ~ I am ~ I am ~ I am ~ I am ~ I am ~ I am."

The wave of fear eventually passed, and he was still "alive."

Hesitantly, Sozwik began floating along the countryside. It wasn't normal travel either. Instead of him moving, the rolling green land seemed to effortlessly move beneath him.

Then he felt a pull, growing stronger and stronger, like hearing the faint sound of a party while trying to figure out what room it's in.

A gigantic tree, towering above the canopy, slid from the horizon straight towards him. Sozwik came to a soft stop, directly above the tree, about a few dozen feet beyond its proud crown.

This tree was like a column of energy, deeply rooted into the Earth, and beaming up to the ultimate layer of existence. Sozwik was directly in this tunnel of energy, and boy did he feel it.

This vivacity came to a peak when he sensed another presence. Though Sozwik couldn't "see" anything coming towards him, he knew exactly who it was. Suddenly, without warning, "she" materialized in front of him, as if birthed by the wind itself.

To make things easier, she took on the human form that Sozwik had seen the previous day, the beautiful woman in the car. You see, "empyreans" (the Wakan term for out of body travelers) don't necessarily take on any form unless they choose to.

In this empyreal state, they felt not as strangers, no not at all, but as kindred spirits from time immemorial. The sensation was so overwhelming for Sozwik that all he could do was embrace her in a heavenly hug. Their coming together was akin to the dance of a binary star system, a reciprocatory rotation, a twisting bliss of basking in one another's warmth.

"Finally. It's been a while," she said. They were so connected that this almost felt like Sozwik's own thoughts.

"It truly has," Sozwik barely got out as a flood of memories rushed through them.

Together, they fell into forever, beyond the matrix of time and space. Though Sozwik still did not know her human name, he instantly remembered that her unified name is Aurora, almost as if one would recall the name of a family member who had long passed out of physical reality.

From this space of non-space, they were then injected into specific moments of "other" lives.

It was like jumping onto a fast-spinning merry-go-round, sitting on whichever horse you land on for a couple seconds (each horse being completely unique), and then jumping off, only to do it again.

They found themselves in a dark room, sitting back-to-back, with a vibrant glowing spiral of bright blue slowly swirling around their heads.

The glow faded as they became two dolphin-like creatures, in a vast purple ocean, racing each other around a giant underwater pyramid structure.

The capstone of the pyramid became a shine in the eye of a robust, bearded viking, with tears rolling down his eyes, being comforted by a beautiful, fair-haired woman.

They glimpsed another time together on Earth, swimming in the ocean at sunset, drinking in the sweet nectar of the moment as the golden sun dipped into the water on the horizon. They were so connected that both Sozwik and Aurora felt like both the man and woman simultaneously. Who was who faded into cosmic unity.

There was no Sozwik and Aurora, merely a blissful convergence of, not souls, but Soul; not spirits, but Spirit.

As the sneak peek into these other lives faded, Sozwik was still pronouncing the "s" in the word "has." So much had gone into one moment.

They both let out a synchronized, "Wow."

The sensation that permeated their ethereal bodies was so astounding that they literally became the feelings that washed over them: love, compassion, gratitude, wonder, awe and even a bit of adventure.

Even their words were not words, but feelings of such realness that words seem to be merely a distant glimmer of translation from their essence.

"It feels so good to remember," Sozwik whispered, intoxicated with insight.

"I felt a vague hint of all of this when I saw you from the car," Aurora said. "But now I realize the full spectrum of my human-form-amnesia, haha."

Still in a state of awe, Sozwik let out a, "Yes, yes" while they laughed together. The bliss was overwhelming and much more acute compared to the feeling in physical form.

Words were unnecessary for communication and inessential for connection, so they spent a slice of eternity just basking in each other's company. For it was a reunion long-awaited, though partially forgotten.

Chapter 12

Eternal Bond

In the mighty power of their (re)union,

Sozwik saw Aurora start to transform. Letting out the most ebullient yawn, she extended her arms out, and they became mighty wings, proud and golden yellow, like Earth's Sun itself. Her skin began to beam with tones of glowing indigo, as her projected image as a human woman expanded in an auric burst.

Aurora morphed into the form of a dragon before Sozwik's very eyes (well, metaphysical eyes). "Her Spirit Dragon," Sozwik thought, somehow instantly knowing this form.

She had become a truly regal spirit, giant and prodigious, with eyes like a deep blue ocean of infinite empathy. Her mouth curved up to form a slight smile that radiated the profound empathy of her eyes.

Sozwik was so captivated that he didn't even notice himself metamorphosing into his respective Spirit Dragon as well. He hovered eye-to-eye with her.

Sozwik could see that his skin was a jovial orange-yellow, textured like a thick celestial cloak, and his gargantuan wings, which swept into his line of sight, were a sprightly turquoise. He felt the omnipotence of the Divine Source running through him, unequivocally powerful yet radiating unconditional love and warmth.

The world around Sozwik slipped into a world within the depths of Aurora's eyes. It was infinitely more vibrant, more real, than anything he had experienced. And there was an underlying component of pure love that seemed to be the very fabric of it all. He saw ultimate totality. Sozwik melted into everything, blended into truth and merged with all of existence. The moment was eternal (and it's still going on, on some level). As the indescribable swept over him, Sozwik's perspective withdrew to looking into Aurora's big, friendly Spirit Dragon eyes.

He instantly knew that the same thing happened to her. With a slight nod and a smile, they simultaneously communicated through thought, "Everything."

The bliss of existence was upon them. Sozwik and Aurora not only felt such intrinsic connection, but they felt like connectedness itself.

Sozwik moved closer and they caressed each other with the energy of compassion, cradled each other with adoration and fused into oneness.

In this waltz of interdimensional intermingling, they both shot upward, flying and twisting around one another, not as two separate beings, but as a swirling double-helix, ever-rising.

Speed turned reality into a blur of color as they broke into a new layer of reality with a booming *whoomp*.

The ascension of their divine winding slowed to a stop. The double-helix unfurled, and they became a heavenly flower. It's impossible to grasp this with the human brain. But it was a flower that reached far beyond the physical realm. A being of such divine perfection that the geometries encoded within birthed the blueprints of universes. Sozwik and Aurora had become this flower.

Their energetic bodies blended together, like pouring angelic liquids in the cup of the divine and happily stirring them.

Their flowered mixture of self went into communication mode, as if two people could both listen to the thoughts of one, like they were listening to a radio.

Everything about their physical lives was revealed to each other. For this information was most pertinent.

Chapter 13

Aurora's Story

Aurora was what we humans would call a psychic in this lifetime.

Truthfully all humans are (and all sentient beings in general). It's just that these senses have been vehemently repressed by The Guard. She was also clairvoyant, meaning that she could see things far beyond the range of natural human vision, including objects on the other side of the planet at times. These inherent abilities allowed her and Sozwik to meet up, non-physically.

Within this Earthly body, Aurora was known as Jenny.

Jenny was born in the state of New Jersey of the United States, right outside of New York City. Her father was involved in banking and her mother was a first-grade teacher.

By the time Jenny was about five years old, she noticed that she was different than most people. She could see and sense things that others couldn't.

Ω

One experience of hers, which occurred on the night before her fifth birthday, really stuck with her.

Her parents had gotten into the most heated argument she had ever seen. Terrified that her parents, her protectors, were now monsters, Jenny ran to bed alone, afraid and disillusioned. She clutched onto her favorite stuffed animal, a unicorn named Gabrielle, and began to cry tears of hopeless desolation. In the midst of her tears, she felt a gentle hand touch her on her forehead.

Thinking it was her father, she jerked away in fear, only to realize that it was not her father at all, but a peculiar man standing in front of her. This man had a caring, feminine touch, but was strong beyond belief and emitted such compassion that Jenny's tears of sadness were instantly transmuted into tears of joy.

He wore a dazzling white robe and had enormous golden wings behind him. Floating above his head was a magnificent, glowing orb.

Then he spoke, not in words, but in telepathy, mind-to-mind and soul-to-soul.

"Everything's gonna be alright, love. Whenever you feel like life isn't going the way you wanted, just go into your heart. Feel the gratitude in your heart for simply being you, a wonderful aspect of the divine. Feel this deeply and fear, sadness and pain cannot exist. Feel the overwhelming love in your heart. From here you connect to all the love of existence."

With his calming hand still upon her forehead, Jenny took a few deep breaths and brought her consciousness into her heart. She was flooded with gratitude, love, and peace far beyond anything she had ever felt before.

Then the mysterious glowing man hugged her, wrapping her in a blanket of unconditional love, and disappeared.

Jenny sat up in her bed, completely overwhelmed by wonder and amazement. This state of awe then gave way to a profound feeling of forgiveness toward her parents. Jenny drifted on the currents of compassion into a peaceful sleep filled with pleasant dreams.

The next morning, her parents woke her up, together, with more warmth and affection than they had ever shown before. Something had shifted. This became the beginning of the best birthday that she can remember.

Ω

Though her parents were loving, for the most part, every time Jenny tried to tell her parents about her mysterious encounter that night, she was quickly dismissed.

They always told her to not talk about seeing spirits or that she was making it up. Truthfully, they didn't really believe it to be possible themselves. They were so immersed in their world of five-sense perception (or deception). Also, they had images to maintain in the community and didn't want anyone knowing that their daughter was talking to spirits.

Both of her parents had been raised as good "God-fearing Christians" but strayed away from the church in their early adulthood, realizing the Church was distorting truth for purposes of control. But they did so with resentment and bounced to the other extreme of rigid atheism. "If it's not measurable and proven by science, it doesn't exist," her father would often say in that typical cynical tone he used when asserting a logical point. Little did he know that humans have far more than five senses. And science has been systematically confined to the study of solely physical phenomena due to the vested interests of The Guard to stifle human potential.

"She'll get over it," her mom would say. "She's just got a big imagination."

Everyone around her (parents, aunts, uncles, older cousins, friends…etc.) repeatedly told her that what she was experiencing wasn't real. This reinforced a false reality which was contrary to her genuine experiences and created a chasm of confusion, a fjord of fear in her mind. Over the years, Jenny slowly withdrew into the shell of Dictated Reality.

Psychic abilities can't be completely repressed, of course, so they would still come up sporadically, especially if she was in any extremely emotional state.

Like the night of her ballet recital when her dad actually left work early to come see it (he never left work early). He also bought flowers and ice cream cake for her (her favorite). Seven-year-old Jenny cried tears of joy as her daddy gave her these tokens of his love and appreciation at their kitchen counter. And when she opened her eyes, misty as they were, she could see, clear as day, angels and various friendly spirits lining the room in celebration.

Sometimes Jenny would travel out of her body when she was sleeping. She knew that it was real because she could watch people and confirm what they were doing later, like she did with her friend Stephy one time in first grade (but that's another story). But again, as the external influences compounded and the pressure to "grow up" grew, she convinced herself that these were all just dreams and coincidences.

When Jenny was about 12 years old, she literally went to another planet when her physical body was daydreaming in math class.

This planet was very similar to Earth, but it wasn't Earth. She zoomed in on a valley, green and luscious and surrounded by majestic mountains.

Zooming in further, she came upon a creature, eerily human-like, yet bigger and covered in dark-brown hair. This figure was sitting in the wilderness, alone and weeping. Feeling sympathetic towards this being, Jenny stroked its cheek, which was like a comforting breeze. The creature lifted its head up, and tears turned to hope. The look in its eyes was profound, and through them Jenny fell back into her desk.

Ω

Jenny's adult life was far less magical than what she had experienced throughout childhood. Magic is everywhere, always, but the walls of denial blocked the vast majority of it from ever reaching her mind.

By the time she graduated college, her abilities had been completely suppressed, save for some anomalous moments.

The constant conditioning by those around her, though well-intentioned, and society at large, had molded Jenny into a hollow version of her authentic self. She had all of the external accolades; beauty, intelligence and a well-paying career as a lawyer, but she was empty inside.

Her career, as a lawyer in Los Angeles, was so unfulfilling that Jenny was forced into soul searching. The only other option was nagging unfulfillment and a one-way ticket to deep depression. She was overworked and mentally, emotionally, and spiritually drained. She had slept under her desk twice, pulling all-nighters on a drawn-out and pointless case that her boss had told her to take on. She vowed to quit after the third all-nighter. The third occurrence came, and she quit the next day.

Having free time was a shock to her and intimidating at first, as she had kept herself busy every minute since childhood.

But Jenny joined a yoga studio, where she learned about various meditation practices along with the practice of yoga itself.

Being someone who tackles everything with full force, she devoted herself to an hour a day of deep meditation. By the second session, she was having the kind of glimpses she had as a child. At this point in her life, she had firmly classified all her spiritual experiences as "just her imagination." But a deep truth had been reawakened and she now understood that her childhood experiences were very real indeed.

With newfound curiosity and nothing to lose, Jenny continued her meditation practice. There was still a lingering hesitation though. The deeper she went, the more aware she became of a feeling of being watched. She had vaguely felt it throughout the last few years, but it was like a distant, obscure phantom, not worth paying attention to. Yet now, it felt as though she was always being stared at. Up close, by something unseen and ubiquitous. It was deeply disconcerting.

One day Jenny decided to face this unseen foe head on during a deep meditation. When the feeling of being watched was at its pinnacle, she broke through her urge to "run the other way" and energetically leaned right into it. It seemed like this force, whatever it was, was more surprised than her, as it appeared to rely on other's fears instead of any genuine power. In her boldness, Jenny had completely caught this watcher, or watchfulness, off guard, and it "fled," leaving behind an ethereal vault of disclosure. Right after leaning into this nebulosity, she was inundated with insight…

Ω

As she and Sozwik communed in the higher realms, it was apparent that this force that was disclosed to Jenny was in fact The Guard (or some facet of it).

Jenny/Aurora had learned much about The Guard. This was all relayed to Sozwik as they were united as the divine flower. It was eerily similar to Paupo's discourse about what the human shaman revealed to him. The themes were the same; Quondam humans of ages past, Trakul/Naki, DNA experimentation, The Guard being a parasite, seeking full control of Earth…etc.

On Earth as Jenny, this information was overwhelming. She had no points of reference whatsoever to be able to wrap her head around this multi-dimensional disclosure. It was a knowing beyond the barrier of the reality she thought possible. But now, as everything revealed itself through the supernal truth of the divine flower, it all became crystal clear.

In this state of grace, Aurora had also learned much about the nature of reality and her purpose while playing the part of Jenny. But all the details she gleaned were still being assimilated. It was almost too much for the human mind to process at once. While everything was evident now (as Aurora), it felt like groping in the dark from the perspective of Jenny. She knew all of this to be there, yet the puzzle pieces were shadowy and elusive. Indeed, it is extremely difficult to bring such insight into the physical realm, like catching a whale shark while fishing from a kayak and hauling it back to shore.

Ω

The divine flower opened and Aurora and Sozwik rolled down through their Dragon Spirits before making an abrupt stop in their etheric bodies, hovering again above the mighty tree.

"It was you who I saw sitting in sadness that day," exclaimed Aurora. "I couldn't help but comfort you." The communication was still unspoken and instantaneous.

Sozwik, brimming with realization himself, responded, "It was as if an angel stroked my cheek. And it turns out to be true."

The eternal moment vibrated like a giant transcendental bell of love. Swirls of bright colors enveloped them.

Aurora smiled and the sunlight seemed to shine brighter. "Fate lined us up on the road," she said.

"Yes. We both felt it, though neither could explain the feeling. And we serendipitously ended up here," Sozwik added.

Aurora explained her journey. It wasn't like it needed explaining now, but the expression on this level felt right…

"I was learning remote viewing. That's what brought me here. Once my perception expanded beyond my physical body, it was just like I was pulled in this direction, pulled to you."

Aurora's attention turned back to her life as Jenny. "I've felt as if I've been watched for the last few months. Most of it just feels like a presence, staring me down at all times. It's unnerving. When I was driving, right before I saw you, I thought I saw a black car following me. Now I'm realizing that The Guard is somehow tracking both of us. How it does this… I don't know for sure. We must stay vigilan…"

Before Aurora could finish her sentence, she zoomed backwards over the horizon in a streak of light. Sozwik instantly felt, knew and understood that she was hastily pulled back into her physical body. "Whatever that was, something threw her out of her meditation."

Fear rippled through him. Overcome by it, Sozwik crash landed back to his own physical self in a state of confused disillusionment. As the confusion settled, it gave way to a wave of hysteric worry, anxiety and fear.

He couldn't tame his mind. Thoughts were running through his brain like a panicked stampede of mammoth beasts.

"Aurora? Jenny? What had happened? Is she ok? Did The Guard invade her home? Could they do that? And for what reason? Maybe she needs my help. What do I do from here? How do I even find her? Ahhhh!"

Chapter 14
Running from The Guard

Sozwik was snapped out of his troubled thoughts and back into his own body by the ominous sound of stomping boots nearby.

He sat frozen in fear. At least a dozen pairs of feet rumbled toward him. The steps came closer and closer. "It's like they're out for me," Sozwik thought. "And they know exactly where I am." In a rush of frustration, Sozwik's eyes darted to the Top Rank Badge, still constricting his ankle. "I forgot about this fell piece of machinery! They've really tracked every step of mine!"

Sozwik was thrown off-center. Yet he also knew that there was no time to think and plot a solution with the analytical mind. Digging into the very roots of his Wakan meditation practices, Sozwik let the waters of his mind become still until the surface gleamed with crystal clear clarity.

Each heartbeat of his became an eternity. In the space between breaths, which was an infinitude in itself, Sozwik put the puzzle pieces together to grasp the scope of his predicament.

His senses reached out and he found that these were Harka after him. They rarely stepped foot on Earth. The Harka only came to carry out the grunt-work of The Guard to strong-arm those labeled as dissidents.

"I guess I'm a dissident," Sozwik thought to himself sarcastically. "They probably didn't expect this kind of unpredictable behavior. The Top Rank was supposed to be the most thoroughly indoctrinated, but Goa and I had some tricks up our sleeves."

Ω

Sozwik's mind filed through everything he learned from Uncle Paupo, Aurora and his lifelong Wakan training with Goa. Still, nothing seemed useful in this desperate predicament.

The Guard kept close tabs on all the Earth-bound Jyoti. Sozwik was no exception. Plus, Sozwik had probably been involved in more "suspicious" activity than any other Jyoti. But that's the risk one always takes when stepping outside of the imposed box.

Sozwik viewed the situation like a painting. There he was in the foreground, seated, eyes closed with a curious mixture of worry and sly Wakan mastery upon his brow. Dense shrubbery hugged him, and trees hung overhead. It was as if the plants were attempting to protect him from the other humanoid creatures in the picture. Not far away, there was a circle of about 14 Harka closing in on him. They were brutish and terrifying to look at; all seeming to be in motion magnetized toward the center point of the seated Jyoti in the middle. The background of mountains and semi-clouded sky gave the image a climactical overtone, which then permeated Sozwik's consciousness.

He would have to pull a Wakan miracle to make it out of this alive. He was cornered and his options had now dwindled to two.

It would have to be either a physical escape or willingly consent to his own capture. As a proud Wakan, the choice was self-evident.

Ω

Sozwik's entire strategical discourse took place within the sound of a rattling branch shaken by the approaching menace.

The Harka were so close he could hear them breathing. They had him encircled. Stealth was no longer an option. He casted his thoughts aside, leapt from the heights of his mind and trusted his body with bold faith.

A voice boomed in Sozwik's head: "Go!"

Sozwik instinctively erupted onto his feet, lunged at the nearest Harka — and before the brute knew what hit him — grabbed him by the waist and threw him at another. They crashed together and tumbled into a gulley like giant tangled rag dolls. The rest formed a line and drew down upon him. Sozwik, crouched with one hand pillared into the ground, let out a deafening scream and sprung at them with full speed. Never facing the stupefying prowess of a cornered Jyoti before, the Harka shuddered in fright. As soon as they flinched, Sozwik launched into a front-flip, soaring over their heads and hit the ground running downhill.

Sozwik tore through the wilderness like a blur, not looking back. He became like an asteroid, unconscious to everything but movement itself, and instead of space, he hurtled through the woods with a silent roar. As the adrenaline began to fade, Sozwik's senses slowly recovered. He heard the awkward clamoring of the Harka giving chase, but it grew more and more distant.

"Should I have killed them?" Sozwik thought. But this question seemed idiotic as soon as it came up. He himself would rather die than have blood on his hands. And he would've been in the same position he was in now had he killed them anyway.

Pressing forward, more thoughts began to enter Sozwik's mind. "The Guard has kept a closer eye on me than I ever thought. But how did the Harka get there? There must be a spaceship…"

His thoughts halted. "A spaceship!" He said aloud to himself, almost trembling with fear, realizing that the Harka were a mere diversion.

Knowing the cunning game of The Guard at play now, Sozwik looked up and saw just what he expected, a spaceship silently hovering directly over him.

In a wild frenzy, Sozwik blasted through dense thickets with reckless abandon. He probably would have looked like a living cannon ball to the human eye. But no matter his speed nor the terrain, the spaceship hung overhead like a metallic cloud of impending doom.

Then, like the reverse of how he came to Earth, a white light engulfed him.

Chapter 15
The Vigil

Seren was stirring with suspense.

The intensive training of the elders was providing the glimmer of hope the Jyoti needed. Many of the youth had undergone significant deprogramming. They were also able to enter the vision-space with the right guidance and supervision. Wogo, who had a knack for Wakanry, was even able to travel out of his body at times.

This led to the Jyoti to begin exploring options they had never previously entertained.

All routes to freedom seemed to congregate around the forcefield fences surrounding the Jyoti's valley. The Jyoti had never been able to even go near them under the watchful eye of The Guard.

Also, every elder learned in Wakanry had been focused on either teaching, deprogramming or communicating with those on Earth. Escape had never even been an option because the Jyoti lived in this valley since the very beginning of their Ourstory. "The fish will be the last to learn of water," they say.

The idea came to Goa when he was facilitating an out of body journey with Wogo. Wogo came back and commented on how ominous the metal pillars were that acted as the connecting points of the forcefield fence.

"The pillars...." Goa said in deep thought. "Aha! There must be a way to shut down the forcefield through those pillars."

"But how?" asked Wogo inquisitively.

Goa responded with hopeful confidence. "We shall find out."

For the next few days, while the rest of the team held down the vision-space as best they could, Goa and Wogo devoted all their time to leaving their bodies and exploring forcefield fence and its pillars.

After much investigation, they had learned this much...

In the ethers, Goa could see waves entering the pillars from off-planet. The fences were activated remotely, probably from one of The Guard's ships. The Jyoti had always speculated but now it was confirmed.

The pillars were sleek and had no buttons or toggles to physically destroy. And they were so enormous that it would take a small army to bring down. An assault on the pillars would just get everyone killed.

As Goa and his five students gathered one night, he began to think out loud...

"Turning the forcefield off or destroying the pillars don't seem like viable options right now. Maybe if we had advanced laser weapons, but the Jyoti are the Jyoti because we've never had to resort to weaponry. Plus, not one of us knows anything about the kind of weapons it would take to shoot a spaceship out of the sky or demolish of those pillars.

We can't go over it either. That thing is hundreds of feet high. And the cliff faces are pure rock so we can't go und...

Wait!

Sozwik! He told me he snuck out of the valley once! I paid no mind to it at the time. I thought he was pulling my leg. But he casually mentioned that he found a secret tunnel.

I have to reach him!"

Goa broke out of his calm state and started running around the room like a nycono with anxiety. His students stared at their teacher in bewilderment.

Wogo, the ever-inquisitive, asked what any critical-thinking individual would ask: "First of all, how do we know he's telling the truth about his escape? Also, how will we find it? No one has even heard from Sozwik in days. And do we expect the entire village to sneak through one little passageway?"

Goa retorted:

"I have tremendous faith in Sozwik. I've known him for many years, and he surpasses my skills in many ways. I will communicate with him, by any means necessary, even if I have to ethereally travel to Earth myself. (This was an exaggeration of course, because traveling out of body to other planets uses so much energy that everyone who had previously tried it had caused death to their physical body in the process and became ever-roaming spirits. Some Wakans, however, still believed this feat to be possible.)

And regarding sneaking the whole village out… Does anyone have a better plan?

Honestly, I don't even know what we'll do when we get everyone out, but it will sure as hell throw The Guard for a loop. Plus, a free-roaming, deprogrammed Jyoti is more dangerous than that parasite ever imagined."

Now everything took a backseat for the order of connecting with Sozwik, roamer of Earth. Calling a council meeting would be senseless until Goa knew that this idea was even possible. With that, Goa shifted gears and devoted his efforts into making sure each of his students could stay within the vision-space for significant periods of time.

Since they all had already been in the vision-space repeatedly at this point, it was only a matter of deepening the groove. They all showed great potential and were quick learners, which is why they were selected by the council to begin with. Throughout their training, each of them anxiously kept an eye out for Sozwik whenever in the vision-space, but he still wasn't heard from.

Soon they all could hold their own in the vision-space, so Goa and his students held a vision-space vigil each night, hoping to cross paths with Sozwik. When Abeo, Bena, Zaltana, Kuwa and Wogo went to the zapixion mines during the day, Goa remained in the vision-space by himself.

Olea and Fala were always there too. Goa revealed his idea to them while training his students in the vision-space. Thinking it a bit farfetched, but trusting Goa's instincts, Olea and Fala provided any aid and input they could. No one else had a plan, so Goa's plan was the best by default.

The two elder-women also expressed concern that no Earth-bound Jyoti had gone back into the vision-space since the council meeting. Not even Uncle Paupo.

"Strange happenings are likely brewing on Earth," said Fala.

This left Goa a bit disconcerted, but at the same time more determined to reach Sozwik and find out about this hidden passageway. In all his days, Goa had never heard of this passageway. How Sozwik found it, he couldn't even guess. Maybe it was an ancient secret whose lore was lost somewhere along the line.

Goa passed the next few days enthralled in the vision-space, leaving only once to give his physical body some water.

"Can't be leaving this ole thing yet," He giggled to himself while patting his body with amusement.

At this point, Sozwik's parents had become part of this vigil also, as it pained them to sit on the sidelines and doing nothing while their son's fate was a worrying mystery. Each night, Anda and Macha walked the vision-space with the rest of the crew.

Anda and Macha revealed to Goa that Sozwik had told them about his escape as well. The three of them were aghast at how their own limited sense of possibility had not given Sozwik's daring move the consideration it deserved, until now.

"At least we're taking it seriously now. Better late than never," Macha said in an attempt to lift the collective mood.

In their waiting, the group learned much of each other, and through mutual support traded their worries for hope.

Ω

Anda and Macha told stories of Sozwik to the group. It was the best way to alleviate the pain of the excruciating uncertainty of their son's life.

Anda, smiling through tears, told a story of when Sozwik was a mere infant. "I remember one time, when Sozwik was not even a year old, he went missing. We had company over that day; both of our parents, Goa and a few other Wakan elders. It seemed I only turned my head and Sozwik disappeared. I sprung up with worry and started frantically searching for him and everyone joined in. I eventually went outside onto our deck and buried my head in my hands, crying. But then I heard a giggle coming from above. Looking up to my amazement, there he was. Sozwik was at the very top of the tree, looking down and laughing. None of us were light enough to climb that high, so we had to coax him down with some sweet treats. But that's my Sozwik. Mr. Exploration."

Macha shared a story as well. If there were stories to be told, Macha the jokester always had to be center stage.

"This one was just a few years ago. I was in deep meditation, sitting alone in our little meditation room. For some reason, I was getting visions of Earth. It seemed genuine too, from what I had heard from Uncle Paupo and them. Anyway, when I finally opened my eyes again, I saw that I was surrounded by plants with an Earthly landscape in front of me. This confused the hell out of me! I closed my eyes and then opened them again, hoping to be back in my meditation room. But no! It was all still there! I did this a few times, almost driving myself crazy, when I finally decided to get up. As I stood up, I saw that I really was in my meditation room. But there were large plants all around me and a giant, meticulously detailed painting directly in front of me, which looked so real when I was seated and viewing it through the plants. Then I heard a giggle. I looked over and there was Sozwik, laughing hysterically in the corner, pointing and laughing at me. My stupefied face must've been quite the sight to see. How he arranged all of that without me being aware? I don't know. And he never told me how he knew that I was viewing Earth in my meditation either. But Sozwik got me good there, and the two of us shared a hearty laugh for hours after that."

"Goa, do you remember that one?" asked Macha, laughing so much he could barely get the words out.

Goa just smiled and nodded. Then he went back to remaining still as a deep-rooted tree, with the watchfulness of an owl that seemed to pierce through time, space and countless unseen dimensions.

Chapter 16
Jenny's Bewilderment

Jenny was shaken out of her trance by a violent knocking at her door.

Collecting herself, and barely able to grasp what she had just experienced, she stood up and walked to the window.

"Cops?" She asked herself. "No. How could they know?"

Rationalizing that the cops couldn't possibly know of everything she had seen and experienced, she went downstairs and opened the door.

Without saying a word, two uniformed men pushed her aside and stomped into her house. They turned it inside out, searching every nook and cranny, as Jenny looked on in horror. Then, after a few minutes, one of the men — blatantly frustrated that they hadn't found anything they wanted — stared down Jenny through his bleak black sunglasses and blurted, "Keep your mouth shut! This is your only warning."

One took her laptop and cell phone with arrogant entitlement. Then the two men trampled out of her house, leaving it like the aftermath of a tornado.

Shocked, afraid, but reluctantly relieved that they hadn't harmed her, Jenny collapsed on her couch.

"Who were they? And how could they know anything? I don't even know what's going on," She whispered aloud while sobbing.

Her mind was inundated with fear. She heard of the secret lists that the government places "dangerous" people on. She also heard of these enigmatic agents that knock on these people's doors. But she always dismissed this stuff as the imagination of paranoid conspiracy theorists.

Jenny felt lucky that she had no physical evidence of anything. She collected no documents, had nothing crazy on her computer or phone and her car came close to, but never hit…

"What was his name?" She asked herself, struggling to assimilate everything she had just experienced. "Sah? Oh yeah, Sozwik!" The interdimensional adventure she just had felt like a distant memory already, though she knew it to be somehow realer than this reality.

"I don't even know how to reach him again. And to think, the other half of my seventh dimensional self is a bigfoot thing in this reality. I would be in the loony bin if I told anyone even a portion of this. A bigfoot!? I thought bigfoot was just a myth. Am I hallucinating? This is too much for me right now."

What bothered Jenny most though was she had no one to turn to. None of her friends or family even knew about these abilities of hers. Since her childhood, she had never mentioned these to anyone, save the woman who trained her in remote viewing.

Jenny met this woman, who was known as Lilyflower, last year. Right after a heart-wrenching breakup with her boyfriend, Jenny decided to see a psychic. She had never gone to one before and was both curious and needed some sense of purpose to shake her out of her disillusionment. That psychic was Lilyflower. Well, Lilyflower immediately picked up on Jenny's abilities and offered her free training in the metaphysical arts. Jenny hesitantly agreed. She had never told anyone about her abilities and here was a lady who… just knew.

Through training with Lilyflower, Jenny thoroughly honed her remote-viewing skills. It wasn't all sunshine and rainbows either. As she became more adept, she was able to see things that shook her to her core: underground bunkers with strange alien-like creatures, dungeons with frightening rituals going on, horrific weapon technologies on military bases, etc. Jenny was terrified by what she saw. She shared her observations with Lilyflower, who claimed to see similar things. All of the alien-control-system stuff was a bit too much for Jenny, but she was still interested in sharpening her abilities. Lilyflower obliged and they shifted their focus away from the "dark stuff" and towards how Jenny's journey of growth and self-mastery.

But now, after the uniformed men paid her a visit, Lilyflower was the only person she could go to. Jenny wasn't supposed to talk, but it was too much to keep inside.

Plus, she had no traceable relationship with Lilyflower. Lilyflower didn't have a cell phone or email, Jenny would just show up at the shop and Lilyflower was always there.

The next day, Jenny went down to the shop, and as expected, Lilyflower was there.

"Hello, Aurora," Lilyflower said with a smile.

"How could she possibly know that?" Jenny thought to herself.

"I know you're afraid. Sit down and let's talk."

For a moment, Jenny wrestled with whether or not to trust her. "It's your choice," Lilyflower said. "…Your free will." With that, Jenny mustered up some courage in her heart and spoke. "Here's what happened…"

Jenny went through everything that happened; almost hitting the creature with her car, meeting him while remote viewing, turning into dragons, becoming one with him, the men coming to her house…etc. It all now felt like a dream to Jenny.

Lilyflower, however, didn't seem worried at all.

"Your story is safe with me," the older woman said.

She continued… "Honestly, those uniformed men aren't completely sure what they're looking for or what you've done. All they know is that you have certain abilities that could potentially undermine the systems of control. They do it to most people with these abilities to scare them into silence. But how they figure out whom to go to is beyond me. It's happened to several of my friends, all after they had a long journey out of body. So, I know that much."

"As long as you're not committing a crime, they have no excuse to detain you. Thankfully we have at least some rights left in this country, though those seem to be quickly fading."

"Ok, that at least makes me feel a little better," said Jenny hesitantly.

Lilyflower spoke again, "So now that we cleared that situation up as much as we could, you've had quite the journey. Reality is strange, huh?"

"To say the least," replied Jenny, finally easing up a bit.

"I too have seen these creatures that you encountered the like of this Sozwik of yours. But I've never been able to communicate with them. Shy they are, and experts at hiding. I caught a glimpse of one many years ago while remote viewing, but never in person. From what I've heard, they seem curious of humans, yet aren't inclined to communicate with us."

"It's all so confusing. I feel overwhelmed with all of this, and I can only grasp little," said Jenny. "What do I do? Should I try to find him again?"

"Yes, it's a lot, Jenny. It would take a lot to find him now, especially with The Guard on his heels. I would say to rest a bit and allow the wisdom of your heart to guide you. Life unfolds in the most unpredictable ways, my dear. But no matter what, you glimpsed the eternal connection beyond the shores of mortality, remember that."

"Mmhmm," murmured Jenny.

Lilyflower put her hand on Jenny's shoulder. "Even I know little about the interplanetary scenario unfolding right now. It seems as if us humans are mere children in this grandiosity being played out. Give yourself a break. Let your experience soak in. You can come back here whenever you like."

"Thank you."

They hugged each other and Jenny hesitantly left. Sending love to Sozwik and making peace with the likelihood of never crossing paths in the physical form again, Jenny walked out into a human world that now seemed alien to her.

Chapter 17
Captivity

Sozwik found himself frozen,

utterly paralyzed, sprawled out on the floor of an empty metal holding cell within the spaceship that had pursued him.

He was lying on his back, mummified, like an imprisoned piece of taxidermy.

His eyes couldn't move either, but from what he could see, it was completely bare, with no windows and nothing inside, save for himself. It was ominously silent as well. He could hear nothing but the sound of his own shallow breathing, which was a relief, as the rest of his body was immobilized.

Sozwik expected a troupe of Harka brutes to come marching in at any moment. But moments passed, then more and more moments passed, and the feeling of imminent apprehension slowly dissipated.

After what seemed like forever, he had finally calmed his mind and he began searching for solutions to his predicament.

He tried to shake his body out of the paralysis... Nothing.

He tried to move his legs... Nothing.

His arms... Nothing.

His fingers... Still nothing.

He couldn't even feel any parts of his body. It was more than numb. It was like it didn't exist. He felt like a rock come to life, conscious yet immobile, and stuck on the cold metal floor.

Try and try as he may, the paralysis seemed utterly impenetrable. Exhausted from this awkward effort, Sozwik was left with only non-physical options. Never had his body been so stiff, and this stimulated more far more fear and noise in his mind than he was used to.

His mind was like a flooded boat. He had to rid it of all the extra water before he could sail - so release he did. After what felt like an eternity of emptying the cumbersome noise of the mind, Sozwik finally felt a sense of tranquility.

"If I hadn't gone through so much Wakan training, I would sink into oblivion," He thought to himself and observed the thought pass by.

Sozwik released more and more until, suddenly it felt like a current picked him up. Feeling its benevolence, he surrendered and let it carry him. All fear was left behind.

He broke through some sort of ethereal smokescreen. And there he was. Sozwik, the Earth-roamer had stumbled upon the backdoor to the vision-space…

It was as if entering a meeting room by falling through the ceiling, at least that's what it felt like to Sozwik. With a crash and a hard landing, he was again among his kin.

Olea, Fala, Abeo, Bena, Zaltana, Kuwa and Wogo couldn't believe their (ethereal) eyes and were all held in a bubble of astonishment. Goa, however, just casually greeted Sozwik like it wasn't a big deal.

"I've been expecting you, Sozwik," laughed Goa.

While still bewildered, Sozwik gathered himself. "Expectations are the fool's income, dear Goa. I don't even know how I made it here. I was captured and my body is frozen in a prison cell aboard one of The Guard's crafts."

"Captured!?" the group (besides Goa) blurted in shock.

"Do you want me to tell you about my crazy Earth adventures?" Sozwik asked, now thoroughly relieved to be communicating with Goa and company.

"I would love to hear every detail, but we have pressing matters," said Goa.

"What's that?" Sozwik asked.

"Since you've been gone, I've been trying to devise some sort of plan, some way, to shake The Guard off our back. The Guard has been pressing harder, squeezing us into its trap. If we don't take action soon, the Jyoti will be fully under its spell, doing the bidding of The Guard.

Intuition pointed me to the forcefield fences. But after much exploration and scouting, it appears that destroying that monstrous thing isn't a feasible option.

However, my mind flashed back to something you briefly mentioned years ago. Something about finding a secret passageway. Am I imagining this, Sozwik? Or is it true?"

Sozwik replied: "Yes. I was so excited to tell you about that discovery of mine. But you dismissed it offhand. I guess it wasn't in your realm of possibility back then. Plus, no Jyoti besides me has ever thought of leaving the valley. Times must be getting desperate very quickly then."

"Yes," said Goa. "The tipping point is nearing. I apologize for my small-mindedness in the past. Even Wakan elders have their blind spots. Do you remember where this passageway is?"

"Not exactly," Sozwik muttered with a hint of embarrassment. "But I do know that it's on the North side of the valley. It's under the overhang of a big white cliff-face. The door itself is a dark gray rock, smoother than everything around it. I just put my hand on one side of it and it spun open. Who could have possibly made it?"

"Maybe our ancestors of old," said Goa. "But for what purpose, I do not know."

Goa continued, "At least we have a general idea of where this thing is. We can do some more scouting and pinpoint it as soon as possible."

Sozwik was skeptical yet intrigued. "What do you plan on doing though? You can't have the whole tribe leave the valley through there? Only two Jyoti at a time would be able to walk through. And do you think you can order every Jyoti to just pick up and leave?"

"It will be a process," said Goa. "But I have an idea."

"What is it!? Asked everyone in unison, including Sozwik, who now felt the warmth of hope filling his being.

That hope was short-lived. Before Goa could elaborate, Sozwik was ripped out of the vision-space, leaving everyone stricken with terror and shock.

Chapter 18
The Belly of the Beast

Sozwik came back to his body while staring at a metal ceiling moving above him.

He soon realized that it wasn't the ceiling that was moving, but him. "I'm being dragged down a hallway."

In the upper right and left corners of his eyes, he could see two Harka dragging him by his long arms. The stomping of their boots echoed through the hallway, accented by the subtle sound of his sliding body.

After he grasped his situation, panic began to set in. "Where are they taking me? What's going to happen? The vison-space... Goa and all of them must be shocked. I'm helpless right now. I can't even move. Ahhhh."

Attempting to gather himself, Sozwik consoled his mind like one would console a small child overcome with fear. By the time the stomping of the boots stopped, he had come to terms with his situation.

Sozwik had no choice but to accept his helplessness, difficult as it was.

The Harka had stopped in the doorway of a large room which was oozing with the energy of a malevolent presence.

"Leave him," said a menacing, serpentine voice.

Sozwik felt his body reverberate when the Harka dropped his arms. He was still relegated to staring at the ceiling. But then an ugly head appeared in his vision, looking at him with pure contempt. It was undoubtedly a member of the Trakul species, the chief servants of The Guard. And this one seemed to be high-ranking, probably the commander of the ship.

"Sozwik," spoke the Trakul through thin, malicious lips. "You've been causing trouble. And we don't appreciate trouble makersssss," He carried out the "s" in an ominous hiss.

"Why is it that every Jyoti who was granted their freedom on Earth had behaved so well except for you? Who do you think you are?"

Sozwik couldn't respond, and he felt like this Trakul didn't want him to respond, instead desiring a one-way conversation.

"We've been tracking everything you're doing. And since you won't be going anywhere for a looong time now, we won't be needing this anymore," said the Trakul, waving Sozwik's Top Rank Badge in a motion of teasing arrogance.

"You've gone too close to humans. And whatever you were doing while you were sitting before you were caught was certainly the behavior of an agitator. We know you Jyoti communicate without speaking."

The Trakul didn't mention that their technological devices were unable to detect that communication, because that would reveal weakness.

"What do you know? Who have you been communicating with? What are you doing? Of course, you cannot answer this now, as you're paralyzed and pathetic, but we will extract EVERYTHING from you!"

The Trakul's anger peaked. "How dare you even attempt to undermine the mighty Guard!"

"Harka!" He called outside. The Trakul, being notoriously condescending, refused to acknowledge the individuality of any of their Harka allies (the term "ally" being a stretch).

Sozwik heard the two brutes come stomping back in, heavy-footed and anxious.

"Bring this wretched fuzz-monkey to the mind reaper! We're going to find out everything he knows."

There he was again, staring at the metal ceiling moving overhead and listening to the sliding of his body on the slick, cold floor. The Trakul obviously had more advanced ways of transporting immobilized bodies, but this was all wicked theatrics and part of their game.

Sozwik soon found himself in a dark room, with a brooding blue light on one side that seemed to be coming from a machine. The machine emitted a low, dull hum that sounded like dread itself. The Harka dropped his arms and went over to the machine.

As he lay at the threshold of the room, the suspense almost swallowed him whole. "What in the Universe is that thing?" Sozwik thought to himself as fear rushed over him like a tidal wave.

The Harka grabbed him again, hauled him across the room and left him on his side, face-to-face with the machine. It was a terrifying device, like a giant metallic mantis poised to eat his soul.

The Trakul chief slunk into the room with a wicked murmur. "Hmm, acquainting yourself with the Mind Reaper, are you?"

"Don't worry, I'll get all of the answers from you soon enough. Ha! Ha!" He shouted, breaking into an evil laughter.

The Trakul spun around and sauntered to a control station in the corner of the room, still laughing under his breath.

Sozwik heard the tapping of buttons which initiated a grim, mechanical rumble.

A machine-like buzz birthed out of the rumble and whirred towards him. Then a mechanical arm scooped him up like a rag doll in one of those claw cranes in an arcade. Sozwik saw the whole room spin past him in a swirl of gray. The giant claw lowered him inside the belly of the hideous steel beast, which seemed to be waiting to prey upon his mind.

Sozwik closed his eyes. Fear and anger crashed within like the collision of warm and cold fronts, causing a tornado of utter chaos in his consciousness. The cyclone spit him out and Sozwik felt to be floating, like a stranger in a strange formless land. He heard the voice of the Trakul taunting him. But he couldn't make out any words. It sounded like a distant echo coming from far, far away.

With a sudden thump, Sozwik hit hard ground and tumbled. He was too dazed and confused to even speculate whether this was dream or reality.

The shock of the impact passed, and he touched his body with surprise. "At least I'm not paralyzed anymore," Sozwik meekly reconciled.

The landscape was a barren gray-brown, painfully flat and veiled in a foreboding fog. Before Sozwik could gather himself, a prodding appendage pierced the mist in front of him. Awe-struck, he looked on as it stepped out and fully revealed itself as a giant, metallic praying mantis creature.

"I should've guessed," Sozwik thought to himself in an attempt to diffuse the fear.

The massive mechanical mantis strode toward him, now completely out of the fog. It was titanic, with four hind legs puncturing the ground, thorax like a missile and arms protruding outward like lengthy, death-dealing razorblades. Its head, a sinister bulge, sat between the long blades, with glaring green eyes that lusted for destruction.

There was no doubt about it that this thing came to kill. Sozwik had no weapon, nor did he have the stabilized focus to manifest one. The only time Sozwik had actually used a weapon was in his duel with that last monstrous implant years before. But now, his hands were empty, and the utter confusion of what kind of reality he tumbled into added another layer of apprehension to his situation.

"There's no time for pondering now," Sozwik firmly asserted to himself, cutting out the noise of his fearful thoughts.

The giant mantis stopped right in front of him, eyes knifing his soul, almost teasing him to make the first move. Sozwik felt as if he was in the eye of a hurricane, urges to attack wildly or flee for his life whirled around him like gales of temptation. What was baffling was that he couldn't tell whether this storm was just within him or not. However, it did occur to Sozwik that this was the tactic of this fell beast, to instill such fear in its foes that they would either fight or flee with wild abandon. Once the frenzy of fear filled a fighter, the fate of the battle was basically set in stone. Digging into the roots of his very being, Sozwik stood steadfast.

He firmly planted his feet in the ground as torrents attempted to sweep him away. "Anchor!" Sozwik affirmed in his mind. Then he did what he most feared. He looked straight into the hideous green eyes of the creature. The initial shock was like being hit by a tidal wave. But against all odds, Sozwik stood sturdy as an unyielding island of stalwartness. When the shock washed over him, he glared back at the twin green demons with newfound vigor. But eventually that too faded.

The giant mantis was emotionless. It said nothing and made neither sound nor movement. Its wicked green eyes just unwaveringly radiated that bone-chilling death-stare.

"This thing is immovable as the Universe itself," Sozwik grimaced with intense exertion. "And it won't budge. If I make the first move, it will be out of fear and surely defeat will follow. I must stand strong!"

Chapter 19
Exodus

To say that everyone in the vision-space was startled would be a massive understatement.

Goa regained his composure and broke the heavy silence. "Sozwik is in grave danger. And time is not on our side. We must go about this quickly."

"Go about what?" asked Wogo worriedly.

"It will be futile to explain it all. Zaltana, can you drop out of here and gather the Council as well as Sozwik's parents? We must call an urgent meeting."

"We must also pinpoint the hidden passageway. Everyone else, based on what Sozwik just said, remote view the North side of the valley. Remember, it's under the overhang of a big white cliff-face. The door itself is a dark gray rock, smoother than everything around it."

They all broke out into their respective tasks.

"And so it begins. The window of opportunity is open, yet poised to slam down quickly upon us," Goa thought to himself as he waited for everyone to return.

Within minutes, the entire council, plus Anda and Macha, were in the vision-space. Anda and Macha were noticeably distressed, distracted by the reaction of worried concern that parents feel so deeply. But despite that, they were still able to enter the vision-space and be of help, a testament to their inner strength.

Wogo came blasting back into the vision-space. "I think I found it, Goa. But I don't know if it opens. Can I explore it physically?"

Goa was pleasantly surprised by the expediency of his young student under pressure, a sign of a fledgling Wakan master. This put Goa even further into the zone himself and his decision-making faculties were firing on all cylinders.

"Yes, that would be the only way to confirm it. Make sure the exit exists as well. Use stealth, Wogo, and return swiftly."

"I will," said Wogo and jumped back out of the vision-space.

Goa then began explaining his plan. Everyone else solemnly nodded as he laid out the details and the roles each of them would play. Being in the vision-space, Goa's plan was conveyed in an instantaneous collective communication, as opposed to the drawn-out process that would occur in the physical realms. It was as if Goa was the only one in motion, while everyone else was hung in suspended animation, absorbing every detail and poised for action.

As soon as Goa's discourse ended, Wogo came back booming with excitement. "That's it! I've found it!"

"Thank you, Wogo," Goa said; his voice filled with gratitude.

Wogo continued. "I triple-checked to see if I was being watched and slipped into the passageway like a nycono. There's an exit too. I confirmed it with my own two eyes." Goa nodded, containing his excitement.

This provided the final detail of Goa's plan.

By the time this core group left the vision-space, the plan was well thought out and fine-tuned by the wisdom of the council. It was to be executed immediately. The ingredients were meticulously prepared in the vision-space and ready to be injected into physical reality. The way the plan was contrived was like making arrangements behind the scenes of a movie set, then saying "action" and setting the realm of time and space back into motion.

They all left the vision-space with a prayer and hit the ground running. The day was turning into night. The Jyoti would soon be invisible to the eyes of The Guard's servants. The Guard was a bit arrogant regarding their impenetrable fences (so they thought), so its servants never kept a tight watch.

The council, Anda and Macha had the task of gathering all the Jyoti of the village, while Goa and his five students would scout out the best path to the passageway.

As the entirety of the Jyoti village was just beginning to wind down for the night, the team launched into action. There were about 2,000 Jyoti to both convince and get moving, so it was no small task. The team first spread out and visited all the elders, who understood much of the situation at hand and quickly agreed to help. They then spread to the rest of the village.

Many of the more wisened Jyoti had felt this coming and, though nervous, were eager to take any sensible action towards their freedom. However, some of the Jyoti refused to leave. It was understandable, as slavery was all they'd ever known. The prospect of leaving the valley was scarier to them than bondage. So insidious is the trickery of The Guard.

In the midst of her mission, Dara came across one such Jyoti, a stubborn young father. She presented him with a choice.

"We're probably safer here than anywhere else," the Jyoti quipped. "How will we survive just aimlessly wandering around Seren?"

"Many of us are still learned in the ways of old, my dear. And I can assure you that we are not leading ourselves blindly," replied Dara. Then she presented him with a choice. "Choose to leave now or get the brunt of The Guard's wrath when they discover we've escaped. Jyoti were born to be free, now is your opportunity to fulfill your divine birthright."

Dara walked up to him and gently place her forehead upon his. His fears melted away, and with a tear upon his cheek, agreed to heed her counsel.

The Jyoti were gathered and mobilized throughout the night. Despite some resistance, the Jyoti were naturally quite adaptable, and the winds of change were blowing. Everything they had was made from their cunning nature-craftsmanship, and because of their great strength, needed less tools than most species. The Jyoti also did not accumulate material "stuff" like humans do. By the time Seren was dipped in the deepest darkness, every single Jyoti was on the move.

Goa and his apprentices had found an incognito route to the passageway which went straight through the deep Northern Forest.

"The Exodus of 2,000 Jyoti" (as it was later called) was like a gargantuan snake maneuvering through the valley. The Jyoti's speed and stealth is a sight to see, or not see, because most species wouldn't have detected even such a large group.

Abeo, Bena, Zaltana, and Kuwa all positioned themselves as checkpoints along the route Goa determined to be optimal. Wogo was sent ahead as the scout.

Goa stood on a concealed cliff near the passageway, awaiting the head of the Jyoti train to reach him.

"There's no going back now," he said to himself, wiping his brow and inhaling courage.

Soon enough, the first Jyoti were approaching him. In an almost comical, mutually casual movement, Goa simply stepped in stride with Kera, Lovo and their children (a young family well-known for their vibrant spirit), who were at the head of the caravan. "I always knew you were crazy, Goa," joked Lovo. "But crazy is the only thing that's going to get us out of this miserable, multi-generational enslavement."

"Indeed," laughed Goa as they approached the entrance passageway together, guided by the navigation of collective instinct. The passageway was left open, as Wogo had just gone through, and they all felt the nervous anticipation of what awaited them on the other side.

Goa slid inside and his eyes quickly adjusted to the blanketing darkness. Despite the possibility of leading the whole village to certain death, he felt hope, the kind of hope that arises when one takes inspired action at the last available moment. Goa quickly skirted through the passageway with an equally able trail of kinfolk right behind him, maneuvering in two single-file lines with the kind of nimble fleet-footedness only Jyoti can pull off. Feeling the presence of so many Jyoti reclaiming their freedom caused a wave of warmth to wash over him. "All aboard the freedom train," Goa projected through thought to whoever was in tune and listening.

It felt like they were literally chasing out the darkness, because soon enough, there it was, an inkling of light. And it was accompanied by a subtle splashing sound. The silhouette of Wogo stood tall and proud at the exit, which opened to the back of a waterfall.

"No wonder why The Guard hasn't found this." Goa thought. "Thank you, Sozwik."

He slowed his pace and met Wogo with a relieved embrace. Leaning out and glancing beyond the waterfall, Goa said to Wogo, "We still have the cover of night. Let's keep moving and trust our instincts."

Goa, with Wogo by his side, made his way out of the passageway, around the waterfall, and down the sharp slope of the mountain. He strode with the agility of a young Jyoti, his body on autopilot, while his mind tuned in to the spirit-realms. Goa was being guided Northwest, so that's the course he took. The mountains were smaller here, and the train of Jyoti moved up and down the rolling slopes like a silent breeze, swift and invisible.

Goa's thoughts repeatedly drifted to Sozwik. "What can I do?" he thought, "But move forward and hope."

By the time the first inklings of daylight began to gleam upon the land, the Jyoti had traveled far, but not far enough. Goa's instincts told him to press on. No words were spoken, just the occasional thought-projections of some Jyoti complaining of fatigue. But everyone knew that the Jyoti body could withstand much more exertion and eventually the complaints faded.

Goa led them only through the densest wilderness, with the canopy overhead keeping them hidden to the eyes of The Guard. As the Great Star reached its peak in the sky, a sonic boom rushed through the forest like a wall of wind and sound.

The entire tribe of Jyoti stopped in their tracks, completely silent and still. "What was that?" asked Wogo, breaking the silence with distressed thought-communication.

"The Guard has discovered our absence," Goa responded in thought-communication. "But what that 'boom' was is unknown to me. We must keep moving."

The Jyoti, with a burst of synchronized vigor, sprung forth at an even faster pace. No creature of flesh and blood could keep up with their speed and no craft could spot them amidst the cover of undergrowth. Northwest, they continued, never stopping for rest, for two more cycles of day and night, until Goa felt a subtle pull.

Turning his head to the left with an intuitive expectancy, a pass between two great mountains greeted him from afar. That was it. Slowing to an easy speed, Goa led the Jyoti through the pass. To his amazement, it opened into a valley, smaller than the one they had fled, yet more discrete and hidden.

"The Guard would certainly be searching the entire surface of Seren for us," said Goa to Wogo. "But besides living underground, this is as good of a place as any. Plus, we're probably a quarter-way around Seren already."

A deep gulley lay nestled in the corner of the valley to their right. "That is where we renew what it means to be a Jyoti." Goa emphatically stated in thought-speak to the whole tribe, pointing at the gulley.

Nothing else had to be said for now. The whole tribe knew that this place was undoubtedly their best option. Those learned in Wakanry had also sensed the generous gulley subtly calling to them, as Goa did. When one is in harmony with nature, nature ever conspires to provide guidance and assistance.

The Jyoti flowed into that downreaching gorge with the ease of a stream making its way to a pristine lake. With each step downhill, a shred of the tribe's collective trauma was shed away, creating space for something new.

The vegetation was thick, and the steep sloping ground was natural wall, stalwart and protective. The many mighty trees curved overhead like giant watchful guardians, while the omnipresent plant-life that blanketed the hearty ground greeted the incoming Jyoti with emanations of welcoming kinship.

The tribe soon reached the heart of the gulley, a curving sprawl of grassy land with a pleasant stream flowing right through the middle. It was wide enough to inhabit yet narrow enough to still be completely covered by the canopy and the upward sweeping inclines on all sides.

All the Jyoti, feeling the cover this place provided, simultaneously exhaled and lay on the ground in relief, though they had walked into a world that seemed alien to them.

Chapter 20
Sozwik's Move

The face-off with the gigantic mantis felt like an eternity.

Sozwik refused to make the first move or back down, though his hope was waning quickly.

That sharp, menacing beast still stood there, secreting an insatiable lust to eat his soul. Just when Sozwik thought all hope was lost, the ground buckled underneath them. Cracks formed and expanded with dust-splitting speed. Sensing a crevice rapidly approaching him, Sozwik broke the stare down between him and the beast and leapt to the side, avoiding certain disaster.

Fissures swarmed about the mantis as well, cracking with destruction. It bent its back legs to jump upward, but as it launched, its weight was so great that it shattered the ground beneath it. With a hideous shriek that struck the deepest chord of fear within Sozwik, the gigantic mantis was swallowed by the ground. As Sozwik looked on with horrified amazement, a vicious wind blindsided him.

Sozwik woke up to his body flailing inside of the mind-reaper. The bright lights were blinding. And he could hear the Trakul, gasping in exasperation. Now vaguely grasping his situation, Sozwik bent his right arm and swung his elbow into the side of the machine. It crumpled with the sound of crunching metal and Sozwik tumbled out onto the floor. He looked up at the Trakul, who was shaking in fear.

"But…But… No one can break paralysis. And no one can withstand the mind-reaper. What are you!?"

Sozwik didn't reply. But he did feel a wave of realization. He knew that the Jyoti had escaped the valley and the vibratory result of that action had somehow rippled throughout the cosmos.

Desperate, but not desperate enough to kill, Sozwik darted past the shocked Trakul and into the hallway. Alarms rang. Lights flashed.

"There's no way they're taking me prisoner again," Sozwik said aloud as he saw a group of Harka running at him. He spun around and ran the opposite way down the hallway. The hall flashed by. On his left, a Harka lunged at him. Sozwik threw his forearm up to fend off the attack and the Harka dropped with a miserable grunt.

There was a door at the end of the hall. Sozwik decided that this would be his best bet. With a burst of extra speed, Sozwik lowered his shoulder and rammed the door. With a thundering *BOOM*, the door collapsed, and he fell into the control room.

The pilot and co-pilot of the ship, two rather small Trakul, swiveled around in their chairs, their small mouths gaping in horror.

Sozwik's internal dialogue was a quick risk assessment. "They could be dealt with in a few seconds. The Harka are still on my tail." Sozwik's senses quickly shifted to his pursuers coming down the hall. Not knowing what else to do, he lifted the broken door back up, and with a kick, jammed it sloppily back into its doorway.

Possessed by adrenaline and a burning desire to never be caught in paralysis again, Sozwik let out a roar that made the pilots jump out of their seats and into a corner, trembling.

Sozwik stepped up to the control panel and was overwhelmed by the complex machinery before him. It was utterly foreign. "I've never used anything like this." The Harka were now banging on the stopgap door. There was little time. Sozwik couldn't ask the Trakul for help. They're too cunning and devious. They would surely just fly back to a safer place or send out some communication, even if they did fear for their lives.

Centering himself, Sozwik tuned into to the control panel. Though it was painfully complex, he could tell two things. The ship was still in Earth orbit, though in concealment mode. And he found the directional pad, a spinnable sphere which could move the ship manually. Putting a finger on the sphere, Sozwik was struck down with shock. It was locked.

The Harka had almost dislodged the door and the Trakul were starting to connivingly stir in the corner. With a deep breath, Sozwik broke through his fear and tuned into his intuition. A cool blue button attracted his attention. Snapping back into action, Sozwik pressed the button, and the sphere below began to move. Not knowing what else to do, and shaking with fear, Sozwik slid the sphere downward. "No!" One of the Trakul screamed. Immediately, the ship swung down and Sozwik was flung to the ceiling.

Ω

Sozwik awoke again amongst a scene of wreckage. All he could let out was a feeble "ughhh" as he lay on the ground surrounded by charred metal. The slight hiss that machinery makes upon its demise filled his ears and light smoke sheathed the air.

With an exhale of exertion, Sozwik rolled to his left side and, grounding his right arm, pushed himself to his feet. "They weren't lying when they said that the Jyoti body was the sturdiest flesh in the Universe." Sozwik muttered to himself, shaking off the shock.

He studied the carnage around him. From what he could tell, no one else had survived. But he didn't want to stick around and find out. The Guard would be here very, very soon.

Without paying any thought to direction, Sozwik took off, half-limping but still harboring strength and speed most creatures would envy. As he wove through the wilderness and the threat of immediate danger dissolved, his mind began to wander.

"How long was I on that ship? Did that cunning Trakul tell anyone else of my capture, or did he want to keep me for his own selfish purposes? Was the mantis the over-spirit of that evil mind-reaper machine? How did I get out of that? I don't even know. Goa must've pulled some move because whatever he did affected me too (and probably saved me)."

Sozwik continued to press on, aimless and lost in thought, wandering in a world that seemed alien to him.

...

The End (for now)

...

PS – If you enjoyed this book, please consider leaving a review and/or sharing it with someone you think would vibe with it.

About the Author

Stephen Parato is an author, copywriter, and idea whisperer.

He wrote Sozwik as a message for humanity. It's a story infused with wisdom and hidden gems that are best conveyed through the medium of fiction.

For more of Stephen's writing, and future updates, please visit:

- StephenParato.com
- Sozwik.com

www.ingramcontent.com/pod-product-compliance
Lightning Source LLC
Chambersburg PA
CBHW070500170726
48291CB00008B/2583